THE COMPLETE ANGLER

Being a discourse on life and the art of fishing between *Piscator, Ephemator* and a *Pedestrian*

PRESS HERE BOOKS

LEONARD MARKHAM

First published in 2012 by
Press Here Books.47 Moorlands Avenue
Kenilworth. Warwickshire.CV8 1RZ.

British Library Cataloguing in Publication Data.
A catalogue record for this book is available from the British Library

ISBN 978-0-9570885-0-4

PRESS HERE
BOOKS

Typesetting by Elaine Sharples

Printed and bound in England by
Centreprint UK Ltd.
3 Princes Drive Idustrial Estate,
Kenilworth,
Warwickshire,
CV8 2FD

THE COMPLETE ANGLER

Go, little book, and wish to all
Flowers in the garden, meat in the hall,
A bin of wine, a spice of wit,
A house with lawns enclosing it,
A living river by the door,
A nightingale in the sycamore!

Robert Louis Stevenson

Semper tibi pendeat hamus
(May you always have a hook in the water)

CONTENTS

ACKNOWLEDGMENTS

In recognising the assistance I have had in writing this book, the first nod of gratitude must be directed up the Golden Staircase, for without the intercessions of a few gilded friends, the commission might well have gone elsewhere.

Those friends recognised twin qualifications – an abiding and joyful passion for walking and the natural world and the need for a spiritual transformation, wrought, in my case, through the patient and positive commitment of a very special woman. This book is dedicated to her.

I would also like to thank Mr Anthony K Bridgett of the Izaak Walton League Cottage Chapter for his encouragement, guidance and assistance in helping edit my manuscript and for his enthusiasm and wit in entering into a lively dialogue with three of the most unlikely travellers in history.

Finally, I record an indebtedness to the fine illustrators of a previous edition of *The Compleat Angler* published by Little Brown and Co in 1867, quite a number of their wonderful engravings, with posthumous approval, now gracing these pages.

Leonard Markham

FOREWORD

by the Secretary of the Izaak Walton League Cottage Chapter

I am delighted to be invited to preface this imaginative and thought provoking tribute to *The Compleat Angler,* one of the most famous literary and sporting books in history, applauding its author's deep purpose of raising public awareness about the ideals of Izaak Walton and the Izaak Walton League of America.

The author's narrative imagines a spiritual journey accompanying two 17th century travellers in time – the legendary Izaak Walton and Charles Cotton – well-known writers, poets and anglers of the day who collaborated on the fifth edition of the great work.

Izaak Walton was born in the town of Stafford in 1593. His father was an alehouse keeper who died when his son was only three years old. Izaak relocated to London's Chancery Lane and lived with his elder sister Ann and her wealthy linen draper husband Thomas Grinsell. The boy made the most of his education and diligently worked as an apprentice in his brother-in-laws business, later branching out on his own to retire with a sizeable fortune.

However, Walton's fame lies not with his business achievements but rather with his accomplishments in the literary world. He is arguably the founder of modern biography, authoring biographies of John Donne (1640), Sir Henry Wooton (1651), Richard Hooker (1665), George Herbert (1670) and Robert Sanderson (1678). But Walton is best remembered today for his classic book *The Compleat Angler* which since 1653 has been consistently republished now in just under 600 editions.

Walton's co-author Charles Cotton was born in 1630. The son of a country squire, he lived on a country estate at Beresford in the Derbyshire Peak District, a wonderful trout and grayling stream twinkling past his door. The boy's father – also called Charles – was a friend of notable poets and literary figures of the day but he squandered a fortune during his lifetime, bequeathing only debts and a burdensome mortgage. Young Charles constantly struggled to maintain his estate but having received a good education from a private tutor and taken advantage of his father's well-stocked library, he became a distinguished scholar, writer and poet who was fluent in French and

Italian. He is noted today for his poetry and his translations, especially for his English rendition of Michel de Montaigne's *Essays*.

Much older than his co-author, Walton was a friend of Cotton senior and a frequent guest at Beresford Hall. He invited his young protégé to write a contribution to his already successful *The Compleat Angler* on the subject of clear water fly-fishing for trout and grayling. This contribution was added to the fifth impression published in 1676 – the last edition printed in Walton's lifetime. Since then, the names of the two authors have been inextricably linked.

The Compleat Angler is a book redolent with the atmosphere of the English countryside, linking angling, literature and philosophy. It was conceived in a pastoral tradition at a time of great national upheaval, conjuring a rural idyll peopled by simple and contented country folk who are happy to live fruitful lives without contention. Its pages contain poetry many set to songs popular at the time and also scientific ideas and philosophical musings on the nature of a good life and the importance of caring for nature.

Inspired by Walton's timeless message, a group of Americans set up the Izaak Walton League of America in 1922 aimed at countering habitat loss, improving water and air quality and fostering environmental protection and stewardship. The work of the league is legendary and it has become one of the most well respected and influential environmental groups in the United States with chapters countrywide. Their initiatives now include programmes to prevent global warming, promote energy efficiency and foster the use of renewable energy.

In 2003, the league became aware of the plight of a small Izaak Walton museum located in a rural cottage near Stafford in England. Once owned by Walton and gifted to the people of Stafford for charitable purposes, the cottage was threatened with closure until the league stepped in and helped to establish a local chapter dedicated to preserving the cottage and the legacy of its former owner.

Since 2003, with the help of league members and the assistance of Stafford Borough Council, the cottage chapter has flourished but there is still much to do.

I referred in my introduction, to the author's prime focus of raising awareness about the ethos of the Izaak Walton League. I hope this book will encourage more people to become, in the defining mantra of the league, 'defenders of soil, air, woods, waters and wildlife' and I invite readers to join my own organisation, details of which are at the back of this book.

I also invite other local authorities, angling and environmental groups, businesses and corporate bodies to follow the excellent lead of Stafford Borough Council, leading perhaps to the establishment of a network of chapters across England and the creation of England's first angling museum near the site of Izaak Walton's own home in Staffordshire.

Anthony K Bridgett
Leek
Staffordshire
2012

INTRODUCTION

The tiny roach and the porcupine quill float flew through the air and hit sweet Mirabelle full in the mouth, the maid just standing there trembling in her Easter frock with sprigs of duckweed hanging from her locks. Oh how she howled at her muddy frills! She stamped in a cowpat and sobbed even more at her splashed stockings, uttering enough profanities to make the marigolds curl. But I heard only the pounding of my own little heart and the sound of racing breath. Quivering there in my short pants on the shore of Roundhay Park Lake, I would, at that moment, have been oblivious to all but the crack of doom as there, amongst the willows, I contemplated the sight of my first ever rod-caught fish, the tiny morsel flapping in the palm of my hand, her scaly fire lighting a passion for angling that has endured these sixty years.

I was born in 1946 in a working class district of industrial Leeds, then a grimy, leafless northern town dominated by its textile mills, factories, railway marshalling yards and hundreds of belching chimneys. Not far from the Aire, a river that shimmered with rainbow scums and stunk of chemicals, and hemmed in by derelict buildings and a bombed-out school, my home was number 10 Bertha Street, a tiny, freezingly cold back-to-back house, one of hundreds of similar brick-built homes in the penumbra of Mount St Mary's Catholic Church. Halfway up the cobbles was our shared outside lavatory. I would labour to its bowl each morning before breakfast, my favourite book in one hand and a slop bucket in the other. And there I would sit luxuriating, flames from the gently burning pages of the *Daily Mirror* warming my little cheeks as I poured over my portal to another world, the dog-eared copy of *Mr Crabtree Goes Fishing* – for years I thought all anglers were compelled to wear suits and ties! – giving me wide-eyed imaginings of clean air, crystal clear waters and wild fish. Published in 1949 at a price of five shillings – the book went on to sell two million copies and became the most successful sporting book in UK history – it appeared in my stocking one Christmas and I read it to disintegration. I marvelled at the comic strip adventures of Mr Crabtree and his son Peter and wanted to join them but like the briar eternally stuck in Mr Crabtree's mouth, it was all a pipedream and only getting sixpence pocket money every week, I had to be content with Thar. He was exchanged for a rusty bayonet, the rag and bone man often visiting Bertha Street with his horse and cart to swap scrap iron and clothing for goldfish. Dad christened the beast after watching her blowing bubbles in her new bowl and shouting 'Thar she blows!' The bowl was held in a plaster-of-Paris stand. Open at the front, its sides formed a half circular stepped wall decorated with honeysuckle, rising to a flat belvedere at the back. Here sat two pretty children. The cherub in pink, who looked just like Mirabelle, stared longingly into the eyes of a boy in blue who seemed just like me. He sat in oblivious concentration gripping his rod, its line dangling into the bowl where a tiny float bobbed for all eternity. I looked at that scene for two years, but the boy never had a bite.

But I was smitten and longed to become an angler. But where to fish? East Leeds had its polluted river and plenty of factory goits and ponds with their own technicolour sheens and you were guaranteed to catch something. But alas, not of the swimming kind. Then someone told me about Roundhay Park Lake, an unsullied gem beyond the chimneys, thoughts of teeming fish having me hitch a ride to the local scrap yard on Steptoe's cart. There I found a Churchill tank, its aerial, together with a few paper clips, cotton from mother's sewing basket and corks retrieved from the bin at the back of the *Prospect Hotel*, conspiring to create my first rod. Six months later, having saved up all my birthday and Christmas money and taken on extra slop-emptying work for our next door neighbour, I had enough funds to buy my first centre-pin reel, fifty yards of nylon line, a float, lead shot and a packet of hooks. I was ready, a few worms dug illicitly from the priests' garden as old Father Keogh was snoozing, completing the preparations.

Waiting at the tram stop with my tackle stowed in dad's old gas mask case, I squeezed Mirabelle's hand and felt like Christopher Columbus as he set out to discover the New World. For our two penny fares, we got a rarefied view of mansions with their beautiful gardens and, as the tram ascended the hill, oceans of green. We got off at the park gates and sprinted through the grounds – at least I sprinted – with the gear in my St Bruno tin rattling away. And I stopped at the boathouse assembling my equipment with my hands aquiver, casting out into the lake at last, my wide eyes focusing on the red-tipped quill as it slowly stood to attention. Hardly noticing the arrival of my companion and hardly daring to blink I was detached from the universe but totally absorbed by it. I stared as much that day as my tiny plaster friend, the soughing of the wind, the splashing of a water vole, the calls of the water birds, the pitter-pattering of raindrops on my head and the 'I want to go home!' pleas of Mirabelle all going unnoticed. At precisely 3.11 pm on that June 18th 1954 – I know the time exactly as the hands on my Mickey Mouse watched stopped as soon as the float disappeared and my timepiece disappeared into the water – my first fish became airborne and I've been an angler ever since.

At Christmas time in that memorable year, a copy of Charles Kingsley's beautifully illustrated *Water Babies* appeared in my stocking. Amazingly, I discovered that the upper reaches of my foul Aire, in a fabled place called Malham, boasted fish and little chaps just like me! I spent more winter hours toasting my rear end in admiration of the chimney sweep's adventures. 'Oh, don't hurt me,' he cried looking a leviathan fish full in the eye. 'I only want to look at you; you are so handsome.' Handsome indeed.

I too wanted to meet a trout and learn how to catch him, my preliminary education in this most exquisite art coming in the pages of yet another book; a book that even outsold *Mr Crabtree Goes Fishing* and next to the Bible and the works of Shakespeare remains as one of the most printed and regularly republished books in the English language. It was not so much the text of *The Compleat Angler* that I found compelling

– for a eight year old boy it was verbose, rather grandly eloquent and archaic – it was the illustrations. How I was captivated by those etchings of the grayling, the pike, the perch, the bleak and the glimpses of the halls and taverns. How I swooned at the pastoral scenes of ancient bridges and water meadows smelling of sweet flowers. And how I thrilled to see a drawing of an Arcadian treasure that set me aquiver even more than the portraits of the stockade and Long John Silver in my favourite *Treasure Island*. The reluctant Mirabelle and I had built our own den from orange boxes and tarpaulins on the fly-tipped wilderness between Marsh Lane Railway Station and the riverbank, but it was nothing compared with The Fishing House. A jewel box of a building with a magical Latin inscription above its door and smoke curling from its chimney, it was erected in 1674 on the banks of a river called the Dove in the year the fifth edition of *The Compleat Angler* was published. And it was the place where the book's two authors would meet in fellowship to tie their flies and drink a celebratory glass of sack.

Throughout six decades of angling, my copy of Izaak Walton's and Charles Cotton's great work has gathered dust and has been superseded in my library by numerous, more deeply technical modern books. Its eternal philosophy has, however, infused my life with an ever-deepening spirituality, the image of the iconic Fishing House lingering in my memory and becoming more mythical to me than any Camelot or lost Atlantis. One day, I resolved years ago, to set out and discover its site or ruin on the fabled Dove in that adjacent county of Derbyshire.

Meanwhile, in contented abstraction on my own Nidd, Wharfe, Ure, Ouse and Swale, I whiled away the angling years until 2010 when retirement allowed to me relocate to a beautiful home near Ashbourne. In springtime, I set out from there in excited trepidation to follow the course of the Dove exactly as described in the book by Charles Cotton. And I was overwhelmed to discover that despite previous years of desecration as a consequence of abstraction and ochre production that led, at one stage, to the river flowing a bright orange, all is as pristine as when it was first described and is now under the capable protection of the National Trust. I walked through Dove Dale on a sublime path from the eminence of Thorp Cloud – was ever such solid nimbus so delightfully named? – and on to Mill Dale. Then I entered the even wilder Wolfscote Dale passing swathes of newly planted daffodils and seeing my favourite dipper patrolling the rills. Finally, like some ancient pilgrim, I entered the gorge that is Beresford Dale. The hall atop its cliff where Cotton lived was demolished years ago but the features he described in his book are still there, the river flowing crystal clear and full of trout. But what of the Fishing House? I could see nothing through a tangle of thorn and trees. I knew it was on the Staffordshire bank of the Dove but Cotton's former playground is in private ownership and access is denied. And then I saw it. A chimney! Waving at me from the tangle as I negotiated a bog and climbed on a precarious drystone wall to get a better look, it called to me: 'I'm here! I'm still intact. The hall was blown up with explosives but I gloriously survive. And my own Cotton and Walton will come here too. Their spirits linger and they wish with you, blessed Pedestrian, to tread the banks of old. You've been chosen. Rouse them from their respective resting places in Winchester and London and spark them to memory and a commemorative journey one more time. Go now! And tight lines!'

Man's life is but vain for 'tis subject to pain,
And sorrow and short as a bubble.
'Tis a hodgepodge of business and money and care,
And care and money and trouble.
But we'll take no care when the weather proves fair,
Nor will we vex now, though it rain,
We'll banish all sorrow and sing till tomorrow,
And angle and angle again.

(From Chapter XVI of *The Compleat Angler*)

FIRST DAY

CHAPTER ONE

A gathering of spirits

Sunday. The Feast of St Thomas. Dawn. Silkstede Chapel, Winchester Cathedral.

PISC: Good morning fellow brother of the angle. What a way to confound my epitaph! Look!

Here resteth the body of Mr Issac Walton
who dyed the 15 December 1683
Alas hee's gone before.
Gone to returne noe more.

Little did the chiseller know!

St Peter and the ghost of the Fishing House always promised someone special would come along but as the centuries rolled by I did begin to doubt. And now you're here! After how many years? Praise be! It's good to meet you at last. Following such an age, I'm reluctant to leave the Elysian Fields even for a week, but you're most persuasive. You're entrusted to guide me through the hallowed leas and the prospect is just too tempting.

You mentioned my modest book Pedestrian. Surely it cannot be remembered after more than three centuries? You surely jest? It must have sunk like a lead?

PEDES: No! It dances Master! Like the newly hatched mayfly, it's eternal. New editions appear in every age and in every language, more than six hundred now, every artifice of the printer and bookbinder conspiring to make it ever more perfect.

Your book was first published in May 1653 remember? It was sold at Richard Marriot's shop in St Dunstan's Churchyard, Fleet Street in London for eighteen pence. Surviving copies are now worth tens of thousands of pounds!

But come, more of that later. The Good Lord has commissioned our adventure. I've been charged with a sacred mission and you have new limbs and are newly instructed I believe in the rudiments of modern nomenclature and grammar.

Away now. The prising beams will soon be upon us and we must be about our appointed business. We'll travel to London to meet your old friend Cotton for Walton without Cotton is like good manners without meat!

What a reunion that will be! I'll newly call him Ephemator. Can you hazard why?

PISC: Most apt indeed for May's aerial king, and yes, I'm cheered at the prospect of our adventure. I feel the rising sap in my legs. But before I stir, I must divulge that I'm imposed of a divine condition. You must understand that you're not permitted to ask questions about the heavenly realm. I'm taxed to silence.

PEDES: Indeed. I'll honour that condition sincerely Sir … but in mirth are you allowed to nod your head if the After Life is all that our eloquent clerics preach of?

Ah! I see you grin … and your head curtseys like my favourite dipper! I'll ask no more!

Arise now and I'll lead you forth. But stay close. The world has vastly changed since you departed this life and you'll find some of your old haunts unrecognisable. London is now a vast metropolis, an ant heap of noise, clamour and unbelievable scientific progress. Linked by a road network used by millions of mechanical vehicles, there are similar huge towns and cities across the whole of England and the countryside is much diminished. But I alarm you! Fret not Master. Although man has actually walked on the moon and can converse fellow-to-fellow across the globe in the blink of an eye, the kingfisher is darting still and our sovereign banks are unmolested. And we enter a new era of universal enlightenment where every man may value what is good and wholesome. Goodness is the Northern Star! It's fixed in the heavens for all eternity. All those years ago in troubled times, you wrote of a divine thankfulness for a healthy life unburdened by the drive to riches and the press of conscience. You waxed lyrical about communing with nature and about the simple pleasures of life where like minded men could meet in fellowship to eat, drink and laugh and angle and after sleeping securely to rise with the lark and angle again! My, oh my, the message finally resounds! And here spouts the lifeblood of your great book. As one admirer famously said: '…the soul of a good man still breathes through its pages like lavender.'

A mere discourse on fish and the angler's art would have been so much flotsam on the ever-flowing river of progress and improvement. It would have been a fishmonger's manual! But no! Your tome, despite the criticism of garrulity, sentimentality and plagiarism has survived all the philosophical slights and the modernity of crafted rods and reels. It nourishes the very soul and has captivated the hearts and minds of fifteen generations of anglers since it was published. The famous writer and essayist Charles Lamb drew a myriad readers to its pages with the comments '… it breathes the very spirit of innocence, purity and simplicity … there are many choice old verses interspersed in it; it would sweeten any man's temper at any time to read it; it would Christianise every discordant angry passion…' I hope we three may discuss the profundity of this message on our pleasant paths ahead.

But hark; I digress with a loquacity that delays us. The cock crows and we must venture forth. Follow me to my carriage and I'll speed you to Fleet Street.

And my goodness! I almost forgot to inquire. I hope your new garments fit well?

PISC: Tolerably so, yes thank you, although I'm perplexed by these metal teeth. What's their purpose? And what, pray, must I do with this? Is it some sort of attachment for a kite?

Oh I see. You pull this part up! And this garment ties round the neck. Forgive my lack of modernity.

But sweet Lord! How fast we glide along with not a horse or carriage in sight. This machine is called a motorcar you say? What invention!

PEDES: Everywhere you cast your eyes there'll be more sights like this to make your head swoon. The modern world is truly a wondrous place. Your incredulity will strengthen my appreciation. In the short time we'll spend together, we'll share our passions, the prism of our shared experience and friendship igniting a fire that I hope can blaze for another three hundred years! I'll show you things that'll make your head spin dear Piscator. We'll enjoy and revere them together and have some fun in the process. And through the gentle communion of angling, I hope you'll tell me more of the timeless truths that continue to keep the printing presses rolling.

We'll turn off the main highway here by way of a wayward route into my beloved Sussex. You must know from my gruff speech that I'm a Yorkshire Tyke by birth. Truly, I love my own acres but I left them willingly for this land of salted winds and turf. What pastoral bliss.

I'll stop here to show you a stupendous view of the sea and a flower. From this ancient

Cissbury Ring you can see for miles. Stretch your legs for a few yards and I'll find a jewel. On these summer days, she dances in the turf. I came south drawn by such a flower and an even fairer woman. She's now my wife. My love for her is as rare as the county bloom – the Pride of Sussex. Here, cupped in my hand, the gorgeous blue rampion and here a photograph – a likeness of her rival.

What double joys I've experienced in this county. What exultation! In over six years of exploring and writing about her Downs and sea cliffs, I've walked a thousand miles or more in all seasons and never a yard was tedious. From my boyhood in the industrial city of Leeds, walking has been my passion.

PISC: But why do you walk when you can travel with such ease? And you speak with such wonder of cars, trains and airplanes.

PEDES: I was born to be a pedestrian. Walking was a necessity at first. In the 1950's, the little money I earned as a child was reserved for half yearly visits into town to get my hair cut, and, besides, pennies saved on such extravagances could buy you sweet confections that would keep you sucking for a week. I walked through the encouragingly leafy suburbs of my northern town at first and then beyond with the aid of a crumpled old map that had kept my fish and chips warm. Fish and chips! What are those? You'll have some for luncheon!

I walked and I found a greener land, cool and beckoning. And that was that! I invested in a pair of boots and began to explore, eventually traversing thousands of miles of my native Yorkshire and recording my travels in a dozen or so walking books. I came to love the freedom of walking and the pure country air. In the intervening years, all my school friends bought motorcars or travelled by other mechanical means. But I eschewed the noise and pollution. For years, I resolutely refused the wheel and the wing, earning myself the epithet 'That Well-known Pedestrian'. Truly Piscator, the flying machines you see above can span the globe in hours but I need the brown earth beneath my feet and horizon paths before me. And if it leads to a river or lake, why, perfection!

I'm at one with a pedestrian friend of mine. In 1928, Alfred J Brown in his book *Four Boon Fellows* hissed that if he could constrain even one motorcar driver to smash his engine to smithereens and to rediscover the use of his legs, he would save his own

soul. And here I'm doomed to damnation! We drive on!
PISC: You're surely bound for that sweeter place my friend. You speak tenderly of your childhood. Despite the gap of centuries, mine was not so different. I was born in 1593 and grew up in the town of Stafford way to the north of here. Pater was an innkeeper although I was but an infant when he died. After his demise, mother married an alehouse keeper. What memories of *The Swan*! The sign – such a beautiful creature – would swing and creak beneath my window keeping me awake on summer nights. I smelt the coiling pipes. I heard the merriment and the music of the jugs from the parlour below and was roused to peep and eavesdrop. One hot evening in the month of June, Old Silas spied me in my nightgown and cap, a bony finger luring me forth to sit on his knee and listen in amazement. He spoke of fish and waters beyond my jostled lanes that reeked of the shoemaking trade. And by-and-by, he cut me a hazel rod and fashioned a horsehair line dyed with beer and soot. And he showed me his beloved River Sow. He made me an angler.

PEDES: I love the byways and rivers in equal measure. And what is an angler but a pedestrian with lazy legs? Each finds refreshment in the contemplation of wilderness and is soothed by natural sights and sounds. One needs the wind in his face and the sight of the open road, whilst the other is content in static absorption of every leaf and ripple.

Our angling experiences are centuries apart but your tale is similar to my own dear Piscator although my passion for our sport came more from reading books than through a blessed mentor. But there's something heavenly and benign in a man investing love and experience in youth, don't you think?

Pardon me Sir. If I may distract you from that bouquet of centaury. We'll continue east now. I want to take you to the finest angling spot in the whole nation.

PISC: You speak with such gushing enthusiasm. My aged bones are animated at your zest for life.

PEDES: Forgive me. I'm blessed with such childlike thoughts. I see divinity in simplicity and complexity alike, goodness and perceptions of badness melding to acceptance and a pervading mood to relish and share the precious moment. And sharing magnifies all rapture.

Truly Sir, I cannot contain my excitement at this adventure. I'm so enlivened that I may fumble my words, so forgive me again.

Sometimes I so tingle with delight, tripping and skipping over ground that cannot contain me, that I think the Good Lord made the world just for me!

Pardon me if I seem buoyed by an excited effusiveness. I'm so thrilled to be spending a whole week with two such prime fellows that my bubble and gush, my verbal torrent is like a spring lamb skipping and jumping with joy at just being alive!

My tongue is totally unable to keep pace with a waterfall of delicious thoughts. My unbridled joy is like a runaway carriage pulled by a spirited horse, my tongue never quite catching up but flailing like loose reins. But wow! Let me gather them now for we'll shortly meet one of the oldest and largest fellows in the world.

Look to your left and say hello Piscator to the Long Man of Wilmington. A giant cut into the chalky hillside, he's beamed down from his perch for millennia. Now scan to your right on the other side of this delectable valley and enjoy the prancing of the leviathan's mount, the White Horse of Litlington gazing down on a little river that is full of your favourite chub … and some trout!

PISC: I should have asked St Peter for the loan of a verbal shoehorn so that I might pierce your monologue dearest Pedestrian. But I tease! Your bounding eloquence is sweet music and this golden river needs no words of mine.

But what is this? The water of Paradise. The four rivers of Genesis – the Phison, the Gehon, the Tigris and the Euphrates – all flowing into one. By what name is this serpentine flower known?

PEDES: Why it's the Cuckmere Master. And at its outfall I caught my first salmon under the delectable gaze of the prettiest maidens in the kingdom. It was a fine fish fit to grace the platter of any sovereign and yet I returned him to the sea such was his wild perfection. He lay there gasping on the pebbles, a finny rainbow-javelin flashing in the sun. Full of reverence, I held him gently like a newborn babe and pointed his nose to the tide under the bewitching stare of the Seven Sisters … the most iconic cliffs in England. They inspired one of my poems.

Through your book, I know of your fondness for poems. And I know Ephemator was a distinguished poet in his time. Here, please take this and keep it. I'd like you to have it. It's a copy of my modest little self-published book *The Footprints of Old Plod – Lines from the Hills*. It may entertain and amuse you on our journey and may illuminate something of my spirit.

In the overture, I note that a famous man once said that if you wanted to write with conviction you had to draw blood every time you dipped the inkwell. I feel that this sentiment applies to poetry more than any other form of writing, the carefully weighed and measured, visceral, energy bursting, tear-soaked words of verse conveying a sense of self unlike any picture of character. You might agree Piscator? Please peruse it later. On page 54, you'll read a poem about one of my more exhilarating visits to the Cuckmere.

PISC: I thank you for the gift most warmly. Page 54. I'll read it now if I may?

A Swim Before Breakfast

Apple-cheeked and panting at the topmost yard,
And there, close by … the sea!
Onward, beaming and breathless,
Bounding along like the Skegness salt.

Gobbling up the ground hair a-blowing,
Quaffing and relishing the chill May air.
Running now on downward plunge,
A giddy prance through sea-pinks dancing.

Airborne, the briefest flight to beach,
A thud, a tumble, a gritty roll and up … sprinting.
A beach-sprung-rock-pool-crashing dash,
To surf and splash.
Unzipped, a button-bursting frenzy.

My pimpled flesh ventured to the foam,
Breath-held and braced.
A spring, a dive,
And Neptune's creamy broth caressing.

Tingling and shaking like a dog,
Then dressed on dampened skin.
A race to sweethearts door,
The whiff of ham and eggs tugging me all the way.

PEDES: But we'll not have ham and eggs! We'll ascend the Seven Sisters, passing the redoubt of Beachy Head, heading for my old home town of Eastbourne. When you were a boy, it was but a fishing hamlet. Now, it's the busy resort of people of leisure. We'll dine there as I promised on fish and chips. The noblest dish in the world! Afterwards, amply fed, we'll take the railway train – another mechanical marvel for you to enjoy – and be conveyed to London and our meeting with Ephemator. I do hope you're hungry?

PISC: I should be. Nothing has passed my lips in 327 years!

FIRST DAY

CHAPTER TWO

Hot, golden and scrumptious

Sunday. The Feast of St Thomas. Noon. The Replete Angler Fish Restaurant, Eastbourne.

PISC: Elucidation is required again dear Pedestrian. Forgive me. What are fish and chips?

PEDES: Quite simply, fish and chips are the most compatible foodstuffs in the whole world, a heavenly marriage made in sea and earth. I'll be boldly sacrilegious and risk the wrath of my fellow Tykes to declare that this fried compendium of fish and potatoes excels even roast beef and Yorkshire pudding for taste and wholesomeness.

In your tome, you give instructions for the cooking of a pike, adding all sorts of ingredients such as pickled oysters, anchovies, thyme, sweet marjoram, winter savoury, claret wine and lashings of butter. If I may make so bold Sir, the pike is undeserving of such largesse and the recipe is just too complicated! 'This dish of meat,' you say, 'is too good for any but anglers or very honest men.' If you think that, what, I hazard, will you make of fish and chips? Never mind anglers and honest men. Here is a feast to tempt even Peter from his gate! And did he not anoint the fish you now hear spluttering in the pan?

PISC: What manner of beast would that be?

PEDES: Why it's the fish that bears the chief disciple's thumbprint on its flanks! It's the noble haddock! Covered in a batter made from flour and strong ale and fried alongside potatoes, peeled and cut into finger lengths – you will recall that the famous Sir Walter Raleigh brought over the first such tubers from his peregrinations in South America – the deep-water haddock is the tastiest fish that swims. Try it and give me your opinion.

PISC: Indubitably yes! The centuries long fast has been worth the wait. So excuse me if I close my eyes and masticate in silent reverie. And this is the dish of the common people you say? The modern world must truly be an enlightened place.

PEDES: As we dine, tell me more about your angling mentor. Conjure me a tale about Old Silas.

PISC: Oh, he would have relished this!

I remember the gentleman with enormous affection. He was a very simple man but he was imbued with a grace that countenanced both calm and tempest with serene equanimity. I never heard him raise his voice or say a distracting or discouraging word. His whole manner was becalming. In my privileged lifetime, I went on to meet a galaxy of great men, scholars, politicians, poets, bishops and others of royal and noble blood, but none of them were the milestone that was Old Silas.

In remembering him, a strain of music passes through my mind and my lips curl in smile.

A former seafaring man who never married, Silas lived alone in a one-roomed thatched cottage on an eminence overlooking our brook. With a wooden settle at its front porch and bright and drooping blossoms all around, it was a delectable port of call.

After our first encounter in *The Swan* I took to visiting him regularly, my wise mother, who perceived in her most regular and cherished customer the opportunities for a young boy to imbue his Christian honesty, humour, patience and natural learning, inventing the pretext of a freshly baked pie. Feeling very important, I gingerly walked the half-mile every Wednesday with that varied pastry, receiving a small coin for my troubles and a lifetime of serenity and wisdom.

With me by his side feasting – for he was a generous and sharing fellow – he'd flick his iron-grey locks from his eyes and look out on his garden to describe every leaf and insect. Sometimes he'd snip a rose for tender contemplation, tracing the lines of its petals with those hoary fingers and sniffing at its perfume in gentle rapture. And by-and-by, after a few days of instruction, he gave me my own little spade and rake, guiding my trembling hands to sprinkle tiny seeds and freshets of water, to chuckle at my almost hourly gazing at still barren earth. And when the rains came, we would retreat inside. What a cosy and well-ordered den.

Accoutred as the cabin of some man-of-war, it almost rolled with the swell and was scoured every morning Bristol fashion and swept between meals.

Hung from a beam in one corner was a bleached hammock. Beneath was a buffed and polished sea chest with the portrait of a full-billowed sailing ship on its lid and the names of a dozen vessels painted on its sides. How I swooned at those beguiling recitations! 'Alacrity, how fast she sped! Stout Hyperion, my mistress of the sea! Aloft in your dangled tresses, such beauty my sweet Aurora!'

Also in the room besides a scrubbed table and a brass lantern, were two chairs sculpted from rum barrels placed either side of the fireplace. On its mantelpiece were assorted shells, tusks and angling implements, various nails and hooks around the freshly white-washed walls disporting several rods and nets. But what attracted my attention more than all these treasures was a spyglass set on a gimble by the window. It sparkled even on the dullest days, on every visit drawing this eager boy to its lens to squint and peer into the very heart of the brook.

But tell me, my educated friend, what's this green accompaniment to my toothsome fish and chips? I'm in such epicurean delight, I can hardly continue. What is this tasty glutinosity?

PEDES: It's a delicacy we call mushy peas Master. The dish is made of squashed garden peas. Try some vinegar with that and do continue.

PISC: Yes, perforce, I was distracted. The spyglass. Its barrel was aligned with the bank of a nearby pool where Silas could watch the industry of a pair of kingfishers. In thrall, I joined the spying, those comets of blue reddening my eyes until the fledging. In clamped beaks I beheld the morsels known as minnows, those tiny fish nourishing a sight more scintillating than any plume of peacock. After an exciting cavalcade of eight young birds had quit the nest, Silas took me to their pool and caught a minnow for my inspection. Wetting my hands like some ancient priest preparing his acolyte for the Eucharistic feast, he placed the creature in my palm that I might admire him. I stood in awe examining his grey-green flanks and horizontal bands of gold until his captor returned him to the flow. I think from that moment, I was filled with knowledge of our blessed connectedness with all things. That knowledge became the bedrock of all my angling pleasures.

Silas cultivated my attentiveness, presenting me with a rod and line on the anniversary of my birth. The brook flowed through my eyes that day, my gaze becoming as fixed on a proud duck quill as that Northern Star you spoke of. I angled side-by-side with my teacher, no tangle or wayward cast into branch or bramble testing his patience or rippling that eternal smile. Time sped the belfry clock on those fleetest ever moments, the brook yielding us three plump trout, we two dining like princes afore the roaring blaze. Asleep at last, I was swaddled and laid in a cart, Silas taking the long route to *The Swan* lest the potholes disturb my dreams.

We angled together many times after that first day and I was inculcated in all facets of our gentle sport. Those times were amongst the happiest of my life and I came to love Old Silas as my own parents. But with brine in his bones, he faded, the ague and blurring sight curtailing his walks to our brook. He held my arm in those last days and I lit his pipe and sat him on a tuffet by his favourite pool where he contemplated his ragged *Book of Hours.* A devotional aid handed down through generations of his family, the manuscript was beautifully illustrated in reds and gold. He died with the book on his lap pondering the prayer *Obsecro te* and I found him with his head slumped against a willow. He was buried in the churchyard alongside his parents. He left me that ancient book in his will.

PEDES: Your nurture was indeed well prospered. A man can do no greater good than investing his most immutable treasure in youth. Grateful reception magnifies that treasure a thousand fold, goodness begetting goodness to eternally nourish the world.

Just speaking of Old Silas now bestows a blessed energy on our enterprise and makes my heels tingle in anticipation.

Come master, savour your last chip and let's leave for the railway station. Away to London!

FIRST DAY

CHAPTER THREE

Victoria bound

Sunday. The Feast of St Thomas. Afternoon. Eastbourne Railway Station.

PISC: Unlike the other milling throngs, I see we travel unencumbered Sir. But may I enquire about our apparel and angle rods? Surely we'll have the need of fresh clothing and equipment for our sport?

PEDES: Rest easy. I've made arrangements for all our needs to be attended at our overnight lodgings. The bearded Gatekeeper was most informative about your penchants and peccadilloes!

PISC: I'm indeed most grateful to Him and to your impeccable organisation. But one little trifle does still bother me dear Pedestrian. You've been so kind and attentive since we met at dawn so hesitancy stays my breath.

PEDES: Speak out Sir! No blemish must mar our expedition.

PISC: Forsooth, before I left, our saint did mention one peccadillo of your Yorkshire race that might embarrass us. He warned of a predilection to knot the purse. An exponent in all tongues, He solemnly recited a sacred mantra although He himself was somewhat baffled by its tones and language:

See all, hear all and say nowt,
Eat all, sup all and pay nowt,
And if ever tha does owt fer nowt,
Do it fer thissen.

Although unfamiliar with such arcane language and similarly confused, I do believe you might require some pecuniary contribution to our pilgrimage? And here, I profoundly hesitate. I have no funds but some special coins.

PEDES: Ha! Ha! You speak just like my spouse dear Sir! But dismiss the mantra. It's an artifice to expose the disingenuous, a colourful bauble to excite and entertain true friends. Rest assured that your pocket and that of Ephemator will remain untroubled. I've money enough for our purpose for I obtained a substantial advance on the sales of my book.

Please sit there and we'll enjoy the journey. And whilst I talk of baubles, let me amuse you with a somewhat facetious but quite humorous commentary on your book made by a recent author called Ed Zern.

In his rather intemperately entitled *To Hell with Fishing* published in 1945 he says the following. I'll read the extract scribbled here in my pocket book:

The Compleat Angler is chock-full of useful information for fishermen. For example, in Part I, Chapter IV, it says: 'And next you are to notice that the Trout is not like the Crocodile'. Walton was observant.

In Chapter VIII, he tells of a man who caught a pike by using a mule as bait. Fortunately for Ike, it was several hundred years before anybody read beyond Chapter I.

In the same chapter, he also tells of a pike that bit a Polish girl's foot. Personally, I would prefer this type of bait over mules.

PISC: Ho! Ho! I haven't had a good guffaw in centuries! It's frowned upon in Heaven lest the angels drop their harps. Ho! Ho! Very funny. Very funny indeed. But I wonder what Zern would have made of my biggest ever catch? With the aid of a winch and a ship's cable, I once dragged ashore a pike that had four carthorse shoes in its stomach … and a complete set of reins and harness! Ha! Ha!

PEDES: And, dear Sir, I set off this morning in trepidation, thinking our conversations would be all staidness and gravity. I've known you for but half a day but I declare we share not only a love of angling and the great outdoors but also a predilection to humour. Our week together will be joyous indeed.

Ah, off we go. The train should reach Victoria Railway Station in London within two hours.

Now if you enjoyed Mr Zern's protestations, you'll love this. I've another little snippet for you. I know it's here somewhere. Here, let me recite these sweet lines from *Chick Minor's Diary:*

Fishing issent fair to little boys. Old Fireworks our head marster said Izaak Walton said there never was a more carm, quiet, innercent reckreashun than angling, and when I'd been fishing for tiddlers one afternoon, and Ma had finished attending to me after I got home, I reckernised that wot was carm, quiet, innercent reckreashun for grown-ups was getting your feet wet and dirtying your new soot and going without jam for a week for little boys.

PISC: Delightful! Most delightful! I'm so sorry about Chick's wet feet but heavens, the poor child should not have worn a new soot!

It's good to laugh again.

And how pleasing it is to share the absurdities of life with a boon companion like you Pedestrian. Your entertainments are as fast as the dizzying scenes from these windows and I'm already indebted to you for filling these few precious hours with such kindness and mirth. But, if I may, I'd like to become a little more serious for a moment.

You must understand that readers of my book perceive only a man of sobriety and tender passions. The times dictated my tone. When the work was published in the Year of Our Lord 1653, Oliver Cromwell had dissolved two Parliaments and imposed direct rule as Lord Protector. *The Compleat Angler* was my personal counter, my antidote to all that was divisive and destructive in our nation during that dreadful war. At the time, I remember writing of my regret 'that Almighty God hath appointed me to live in an age in which contention increases and charity decays'.

In prayer and contemplation, encouraged by friends – my muse, the metaphysical poet John Donne who died in 1631 always encouraged me to compose a book on angling – I felt compelled to dip my pen and write of Elysian Fields far removed from the killing grounds of Naseby and Marston Moor.

But puritanical sentinels stayed my quill. Had I with levity written a frivolous or contentious word, then the whole Commonwealth might have been covetous of my head.

Do recall that the rulers of that new England were sober and dour men who frowned on simple sports and recreation. With eyeglasses pressed close, they examined every word. But little did they know that I managed to chide their Lord Protector under their very noses!

As you know, I was an ardent Anglican, my book bursting with imagery and abstract references and metaphors redolent of the religion I held so dear. Indeed, my very title could have been *The Compleat Anglican!* In my minds eye it was! Such a title, would, of course, have signed my death warrant and my book would have been burnt. But have you noticed the arcane game I played in scribing the title words in my front cover cartouche? Contemplate it sometime Pedestrian. The embracing fish are open-mouthed and betray not the secret. But study the lower beast on the right. Engage his eye and he will wink at you!

And in my introduction, I anonymously and cunningly wrote these chastising lines. 'I have in several places mixed … but some innocent mirth, of which, if thou be a severe, sour-complexioned man, then I here disallow thee to be a competent judge'. That man was the awful fellow with the warts!

But what is this pray but a samovar on wheels?

PEDES: It's called a tea trolley and we'll partake of some refreshment. Please, two cups of your best Darjeeling attendant Sir.

PISC: It's both refreshing and toothsome. But glory be! This contrivance is most unlike the coach and horses of old. The beast flashes through the countryside with not a single jolt. See, the cup betrays scarcely a ripple. This journey is most agreeable.

PEDES: I'm gratified you find it so. But in speaking of those troubled times, your reticency hides a remarkable tale that even now gives me palpitations.

Did you not nobly jeopardise your life and the writing of *The Compleat Angler* to serve your king?

Tell me about your most famous escapade during the Civil War. Tell me about your adventure with King Charles II's necklace – The Lesser George.

PISC: Very well but I'm sure history pays my role scant attention in the midst of so much sacrifice.

I remember I was still labouring over my manuscript in that fateful year of 1651. I was nearly sixty years of age by then and my eyesight was fading. I can recall there was a shortage of candles and ink after I left London and went to take up residence in Clerkenwell. It was much safer there for prominent Royalist sympathisers like me.

I received regular bulletins about the course of the war from my friends in an informal convocation devoted to tolerance and peace. It was known as the Great Tew Circle. Our group – most of the others were Anglican clergymen – met clandestinely at the home of Viscount Falkland at Great Tew in Oxfordshire. The widespread reports of clergy being arrested, removed from office and imprisoned and the dreadful stories about looting and iconoclasm in places of worship – the organ in your very own Howden Minster in Yorkshire was smashed to pieces – drove us to kneel in supplication.

But sometimes, even for pacifiers like me, prayer was not enough.

Some few days after the debacle at Worcester – I remember that awful day when our sovereign was vanquished and had to flee for his life – I noticed a man with a lantern.

He was loitering under a penthouse opposite my abode. The hour approached midnight and the alley was still. As I looked up from my papers he flourished his light and beckoned me downstairs to receive a letter. Written in a fine hand, it was from a Staffordshire lawyer, a man called Robert Milward. Knowing of my steadfast loyalty to the king and also of my regular habit of frequenting the London-Stafford road on my peregrinations to my home county, he asked me to travel north to receive a package.

PEDES: Was that the fabled Lesser George?

PISC: It was indeed. In making his escape, Charles had assumed the guise of a lowly woodsman and had relinquished his symbol of kingship. The diamond-studded medallion of the Order of the Garter was entrusted to Colonel Thomas Blague. He was captured in an isolated farm near my old home and sent to the Tower of London. But before the Roundheads took him, with the help of the farmer, he managed to hide the George. I was charged with returning it to Blague.

PEDES: What happened to the king?

PISC: He decided it would be safer to travel alone and set out on foot for Wales. But he was thwarted. Then a stroke of luck. Our plucky and steadfast maiden Mistress Jane Lane of Bentley Hall had been issued with a safe conduct pass to visit a sick friend in Bristol. The king became her groom! After criss-crossing several counties over forty-five days, the fugitive finally made it to Shoreham in Sussex. There he took ship aboard the blessed ship *Trinity*.

I set off for Stafford.

PEDES: Weren't you frightened Master?

PISC: I was a little afeard yes, but at an age remarkable for the time, I was happy that I had enjoyed a fruitful life graced by two wonderful wives and many children.

And I loved my king.

A reward of £1000 had been offered for his arrest. He would have been dispatched just like his father. And we abettors with him.

That hideous Civil War spawned insane cruelty on both sides. But we prayed. Never underestimate the power of prayer dear Pedestrian.

I shouldn't divulge this on pain of a heavenly cuff but I can tell you that we prayed with great efficacy during your own last century for the victims of the many atrocities of the two world wars. And we prayed in my time for the king, for the prisoners who had their ears cut off and their eyes put out and for those who suffered the horrors of hanging, drawing and quartering.

The barbarism of man is not confined by epochs but I can tell you that prayer and a collective consciousness entrained with that universal intelligence that governs all our lives, can move mountains.

And hidden beneath my cloak, all I had to move was a leathern package.

PEDES: Did you return to London unscathed?

PISC: I did. My journey home was without incident and I was unmolested.

Within a few days I managed to contact Colonel Blague's wife, she passing over my package to her husband. By some intrigue, he escaped from his cell. Evading his pursuers the gallant gentleman finally made it to the coast and sailed for France, returning the package to its owner.

I bought some new candles and finished my book.

But I couldn't resist a final swipe at the man with the big nose.

I dedicated *The Compleat Angler* to my good friend John Offley of Madeley Manor in my home county of Stafford. Under all their big noses, he prosecuted our Royalist cause and after his arrest and imprisonment in the Tower of London he conspired with Blague for the return of the Lesser George.

It was John who recruited me as courier to the king.

And it was John again who invented the ruse of the sick friend in Bristol. Mistress Jane of Bentley Hall was his wife's first cousin!

We were all spies and agents!

Yes I had a colourful and an eventful existence. Draper, ironmonger, part time tax collector, author, historian, biographer, poet and spy!

PEDES: And I've been under the delusion all these years that angling was your main diversion. Gentle sport indeed.

Our journey has flown in the telling of your great adventure but look! We're crossing the river now. In minutes we'll be in one of the most seethingly populated cities in the world. Prepare yourself for a monumental change.

Old Father Thames still wends his timeless course but there is little else to recognise from your century. The Great Fire of London provided fertile ground for a new metropolis to take root and Sir Christopher Wren made many designs.

Tell me, did you ever see his magnificent St Paul's Cathedral?

PISC: No. It's construction I believe began in 1677 just five years before I hung up my angle rods for the last time. But I did see the drawings. Sir Christopher gave me a peep one day while we dapped for chub at Windsor. He was a good angler but an even better architect.

The cathedral survives you say? I should like to see it.

PEDES: You shall see it Master. And you'll see another of his great masterpieces, for the rendezvous with Ephemator is in Wren's St James's Church in Piccadilly. We'll complete our trio there.

For now, welcome to Victoria Station. It's named after a recent queen.

Please hook your arm in mine against the eddying tide of men. The Gatekeeper would be exceedingly vexed if I lost you!

We'll descend into the bowels of the earth and be transported under London.

Come, we take the Tube.

FIRST DAY

CHAPTER FOUR

The trinity complete

Sunday. The Feast of St Thomas. Evening. St James's Church, Piccadilly, London.

PEDES: I told you it was but a short distance. Here it is. Much smaller than St Paul's but a real gem. It was Sir Christopher's favourite church you know.

How are you feeling?

PISC: Agitation and excitement mingle me to dizziness. Although methinks it might have been the odour in that dark place. I need your arm once more.

PEDES: Come Sir. I'll lead you to the appointed trysting point under the tower. What could be more appropriate than to wait here beside this plaque honouring a great man?

CHARLES COTTON
OF BERESFORD DALE
angler and man of letters
friend of Izaak Walton &
author of the second part
of The Compleat Angler.
BORN 1630 & BURIED IN THIS
CHURCH 16th FEBRUARY

There. I'll step away into the shadows. The bell will shortly chime its hour. Take these sacred seconds to greet your old friend alone.

EPHEM: What sound is this that rouseths me? For whom the bell tolls … it tolls for me.

My eyes are misted but I see a vision in the gloom. Is that you Master?

PISC: Yes, it's me Charles … we're restored to life at last.

But no! Don't kneel! Arise and let us clasp in ancient friendship.

And banish those teardrops.

EPHEM: My dearest Izaak.

Let me savour the instant and kiss your gentle brow and after centuries of biting regret, permit me to impart three words that have remained as unseen pearls in my breast since our last parting.

Unashamedly Master, oh Master, I love you!

I wrestled with the unuttered serpent as you were laid to rest and I've grappled with the beast in all eternity. But now I utter those glorious words and weep in joy, flourishing the ring that you bequeathed me in your will.

Master, I do love you as a son. You were the best friend I ever knew.

And what joy! If I heard the conditions true, I'm to join a tour of our old haunts, with a hint, if I apprentice myself to your good instruction, of full redemption for leaving this world in penury with the loss to creditors of my beloved Beresford Hall.

I'm the most fortunate man in the history of the world and I'm recalled to permit this holy salutation.

But excitement clouds my courteous inclinations.

Where is the man whose intercession makes all this possible?

Where is he who has allowed me to speak to you as a boy to his devoted father?

Where is the fellow who will take me to own home dale?

Where is this Pedestrian?

PEDES: I'm here Sir behind this pillar.

Viola!

I didn't wish to intrude on your greeting.

Here, let me warmly shake you by the hand and welcome you to our undertaking.

It's so wonderful to meet you Ephemator.

But let me explain why I've named you so. Your nomenclature is that of the mayfly on your favourite Dove. You'll angle there again!

Come, let's press the laughter of decades into this allotted week and be away instantly for refreshment and rest before the morrow.

But one small matter needs attention before we quit this church.

You look most elegant in your modern suit of clothes Sir. I do hope they're to your liking?

EPHEM: I rate them highly Pedestrian and thank you kindly for your attention.

PEDES: I'm so gratified, so pardon my animation.

It's just a trifle Ephemator but, unless we're employed as high court judges, gentlemen don't wear wigs in 2011.

Especially wigs smoking with three centuries of dust!

Let's walk arms linked as bonded brothers along Piccadilly.

I'll hail a cab and we'll speed along Pall Mall, the Strand and your old Fleet Street and on to Ludgate Hill and our inn. Nearby is the towering St Paul's Cathedral. At matins on the morrow we'll go there to offer thanksgiving for our sanctified trinity of men.

Step in my friends and I'll describe the scene as we drive along.

FIRST DAY

CHAPTER FIVE

Three candles

Easter Sunday. The Feast of St Thomas. Evening. Club Quarters Hotel, Ludgate Hill, London.

EPHEM: I turned the wheel as demonstrated dear Pedestrian but the fervency of the flow was most skittish. In one moment, rods of ice assailed me; in the next I was under the battlements drenched in boiling oil. Most invigorating!

PEDES: And how fared you Piscator?

PISC: Oh! I just stood there trembling in wonder. Water in abundance in my bed-chamber, an ice-cave with serried ranks of balsams and liquors, the softest carpets, drapes and hangings to bedazzle any sultan, a couch to invite the dreams of the gods, a speaking tube that had me scurrying in a game of hide and seek and a machine that beams its images from afar! Magic materialised. Miracles! Pure miracles!

PEDES: I'm glad you're both comfortably amazed and ensconced.

Now, the waiter will light our candles? I requested three lights. A trinity of flames to celebrate this special night.

I've taken the liberty of ordering food and wine I hope you'll enjoy. Perhaps you don't get such exotic fare up there?

EPHEM: Aha! You're a poet like myself Sir. Piscator has already acquainted me with your little book. We've not only a love of angling in common.

And talking about angling, I particularly enjoyed your tribute to the trout you nobly returned at Aysgarth Falls in your own North Yorkshire. 'Speckled drifter of crystalled stream'. I like that.

PISC: Exotic fare up there? I'll whisper, lest the celestial broiler pours more oil on my pate although I complain not. Toothsome and wholesome if a trifle predictable. That's my verdict.

But with what meat will you grace our table?

PEDES: Crave my indulgence gentleman for I furnish a Yorkshire feast. Two such indulgences in one day for you dear Sir.

First on our plates, to be served separately from the main repast, as is the custom of true Tykes, will be a hymn in a batter anointed with beef gravy. You'll write a sonnet to the Yorkshire Pudding my esteemed Ephemator!

Next comes the sirloin coddled with roast potatoes, peas, carrots and beans.

Finally, if you care to ease your trouser belts a notch, we'll have apple pie and custard.

And here in cavalcade come our puddings, the chef and his rosy-cheeked cohorts beaming beneath their hats.

Will you say grace Master?

PISC: I will my friend in thanks for a perfect day and the prospect of a perfect week ahead.

Dear Lord, thank you for the food we are about to receive. We are grateful for all the bounteous things that yield their lives for the nourishment of man. Bless our company this night and prosper our endeavours that we three, in turn, might nourish the world.

Amen.

Now let's quaff this ruddy wine and toast our task.

To the friendship of the angle!

ALL: (in unison) To friendship!

EPHEM: 'Tis no wonder our sovereign king dubbed this meat Sir Loin. Our adventure has the finest beginning.

But tell me Pedestrian of your plans. The Master and I are all agog. What of the morrow?

PEDES: *The Compleat Angler* will be our template.

After breakfast at dawn, we'll sanctify our mission with a visit to St Paul's and then on by cab to the spot where Piscator first stretched his legs up Tottenham Hill. For the first two days, we'll stretch all our legs on a walk to Ware following what's left of the course of the River Lea.

Ephemator, as our friend has already explained, my abiding passion is walking. As much as I enjoy angling, if it really came to a choice, I'd forego the rod for the boot every time.

And didn't Dame Juliana Berners, the Prioress of Sopwell Nunnery – she wrote an angling contribution to the famous Book of St Albans in 1496 – say that even an angler with a dry net had the consolation of a wholesome walk?

Yes, I love a path beneath my feet, because I feel empowered with the presence of divinity when I'm striding forth, resonating with Luke's two apostles who shared the Emmaus road with their Lord unknowing. But, unlike them, I'm privileged with the knowledge of that best of all companions.

Jesus blessed each path with his footprints. So, isn't every track across the world a *Via Sacra*? And wont our trinity of footfalls whisper the sweetest Angelus song?

I know we're in good company. Jesus was a keen walker. And he also enjoyed a fine glass of wine gentlemen.

Cheers!

Here's to me and my wife's husband not forgetting missen!

Where was I? Yes, we'll walk along the banks – where permitting – of the long-suffering River Lea heading upstream towards the outskirts of Waltham Abbey where we'll stay the night.

I'm afraid Piscator that the inn known as the *Thatched House* at Hoddesdon referred to in the very first page of your book was demolished centuries past. Fittingly, a brewery now occupies its site.

But fear not gentleman you'll not be asked to recline under the stars; accommodation will be provided for our rest.

The distance from Waltham Abbey to Ware is but a few miles, so, on our third day, I've an inkling to fish – you both cheer! ambling to the *Trysting Tree Hotel* for refreshments and sleep.

On the fourth day, I've arranged for our journey north to Derbyshire and Brailsford. It's there, in the fifth edition of the great book, that you, dear Ephemator, begin the first chapter of your delightful contribution.

From Brailsford, we'll wander through country fields to Ashbourne and the *Green Man Hotel.*

Our fifth day's walk will deliver us to Tissington Manor where Sir Percival Twist will be our host

From there, onward through Dove Dale, Wolfscote Dale and Beresford Dale – you shed a nostalgic tear Ephemator – fear not, all are still pristine! – to our final hearth. And I'll tease you for now and keep its identify secret until we see its smoke.

Finally, I'll take my leave of you in the village of Hartington.

What say you to this itinerary?

PISC: I'm deeply honoured by the opportunity of seeing my banks once more and following our old paths.

You've invested so much thought, organisation and money into this enterprise that I'm humbled.

I know the journal you'll pen of our travels will have the ultimate imprimatur and by the compact of our presence here, I vow – we vow – don't we Ephemator? – to refresh your book and its search for presence and harmony, pouring forth our new enlightenings for your sacred record, offering our thoughts and prayers for the contemplation of new generations.

EPHEM: You speak for us both Sir and I too applaud this venture. Bless you Pedestrian.

As I shut my eyes in savouring this tender viand, so I'll savour every moment we spend together.

But you mentioned fishing? Do fish still flourish hereabouts? The million mouths in this seething London – surely they covet every fin?

PEDES: It's true; angling in this third millennium has never been more popular. Some two million fellows – and some women – cast a line every year. But here's the difference. Nearly every fish caught is returned to swim free. Apart from trout and salmon and the occasional pike, almost everything else – roach, bream, dace, perch, tench, carp and the rest – goes back in the water to live and multiply. The watchwords now are preservation and conservation. Today, we largely fish for sport – not for the pot. And after centuries of despoliation, abstraction and pollution, our watercourses have never been as clean. And you Piscator, you helped the grand awakening. Your visions of an esteemed and exalted Arcadia stuck a chord with all conscious men. Your gentle persuasions dispelled all superior detachments for more lofty realisations of connectivity and mutual dependency. Visionaries like you began an environmental movement that's sweeping the world.

Believe it or not, in the year 1922 an organisation called the Izaak Walton League was formed in America. With a membership now of over 38,000 people – I've joined! – it promotes a holistic view of our interaction with this good earth, defending soil, air, woods, waters and wildlife.

Piscator; can you remember the thatched cottage you bought in 1655 at Shallowford near your old home? You left it in your will to the citizens of Stafford to provide income for a charitable trust.

You can remember? Well, after years of neglect and two disastrous fires, with the invaluable financial help of the Stafford Borough Council and a fine body of English anglers who diligently offer their services for free, it's finally been restored to its glory with roses and herbs at the door. And I'm delighted to tell you that it's now a museum to your vision although across the world, there is still much to do.

I bought something there a few weeks back that should, by and by, entertain you.

PISC: But hallelujah I deserve no plaudits. Pray realise, I began with no passion for crusade. My thoughts were an antidote to the foulness about me. My quills scratched a counter to all that was morbid in that decade of smoke and desolation. I found in angling a respite to death and darkness. It was my solace and succour.

I was an old and decrepit scribe. Weary limbs denied me the field but I could unfurl a standard whose threads mirrored the sun. I kept the light trimmed within me until the smoke cleared.

All these centuries on, it's so gratifying to know that our meagre tome was such a catalyst for change … isn't it Ephemator?

EPHEM: It most certainly is.

I'm astonished at your news Pedestrian although I decline all praise. My contribution was but an addendum and I wrote it in ten hectic days. Our author persuaded me to add a few lines on the art of fly-fishing but I was motivated more by pressing debts than by any epiphanies.

Huh! By the sound of your reports, I could have paid off every usurer and lived handsomely on the royalties for a hundred years!

But know this. I did have a hunger for money but I really loved my angling. I could see the face of God in my own Pike Pool?

PEDES: The Master has already told me about Old Silas and his own angling communion. Tell me about yours Ephemator. What made you an angler?

EPHEM: I was drawn to it like a moth to a flame.

From my window in Beresford Hall on our great rock, I could look down on the River Dove far below, its glides twinkling. Forgetting my studies, I would sit at my little portal watching the clouds scud over Wolfscote Hill. The light danced and slanted above the gorge like scimitars on fire and on the instant of my tutor closing his book, I would scurry down that cliff panting with excitement for a secret assignation by my own Pike Pool. There I'd meet my friend Simon the blacksmith's son. My tutor taught me the arts and sciences but Simon showed me so much more. He gave me back my boyhood and taught me to fly fish.

Jolly and tousled haired with huge hands like his father, Simon knew every stone in our precious valley. We explored together, striding out through Beresford Dale, Wolfscote Dale and the incomparable Dove Dale. We climbed the eminences of Thorp Cloud and Narrowdale Hill, wandered by the crumbled ramparts of Pilsbury Castle Hills with our wooden swords, scuttled up cliffs, built dams and rafts, penetrated the deepest caves with a lantern, snared birds and beasts, quaffed illicit tankards of ale and gorged on fat and redolent cheeses from the market stalls in Hartington and Alstonefield. And, best of all, we fashioned the most lithesome angle rods that ever cast a shadow. Glory be! Simon even manufactured his own hooks!

Barbed and tempered he produced them and a tiny vice in his father's own forge. Then began the real prestidigitation.

We'd woven a rustic arbour on the site I later chose for my Fishing House and it was there that Simon – the ham-fisted Simon – showed the dexterity of the keenest spider, weaving and winding filaments of fur and feather to be transformed into simulacra that would entice the very Kraken from his lair. He'd been instructed by my neighbour and kinsman Captain Henry Jackson of Stanshope who'd taught him well

The whiskers from a fox's snout were married to coot, hen and heron feathers, a snippet of mole fur and a tippet from a kingfishers wing, the intricate confection metamorphosing around that twist of metal to become the epitome of deceit.

He named one fly the *Royal Charles* dubbing it with his sword in my honour and conjuring a trout from my Pike Pool on his third cast.

'Now you'll do the same young Sir,' he said handing me the rod. 'Think like a fly and let the gentle rhythms of its flight comport your arm. Slowly. Like the tail of my master's stallion in yonder field, let your horsehairs swish and fall naturally in the wind and keep your rod erect when you cast. No, not like that! You've lost my fly on the lichens atop the pinnacle rock. Now I must swim and climb for it! But hold my shirt and worry not. I'll retrieve it and we'll try and try again.'

And we repeated the process in graceful harmony, very soon our creels competing for the plumpest trout and grayling.

PEDES: But you hesitate Ephemator, your eyes betraying a darker glow.

EPHEM: Simon was more to me than any dear brother Pedestrian but he died after that first glorious summer. Kicked by a horse in the shoeing, he lingered in pain for a whole week. He was but sixteen years old.

We laid him down in Bentley churchyard.

Just a month later, my beautiful mother also perished of a fever, she too going to the same ground.

After that and I immersed myself in study, contemplation and the writing of my first cathartic verses, keeping a votive flambeaux beacon in my window to attend my prayers.

By-and-by my anguish faded and in the following spring I returned alone to my own sweet pool, recounting those instructions to perfection, memories of two wonderful people fortifying me like a cordial.

And then you came along Master to imbue my castings with even more meaning.

In later years, the spirit of my treasured mother inspired many of my poems and I built the Fishing House on the spot where Simon wove his magic. Above its door I raised the inscription *Piscatoribus Sacrum 1674* and mine and Piscator's entwined initials

Alas, you never saw its final completion did you Master? But I wrote to you of it and you replied.

PEDES: And I have a copy of that letter here!

Look!

It's dated April 29th 1676.

PISC: Well, I'm nonplussed! Not stone but parchment. How could it still exist?

But please continue my friend and forgive the interruption as I wonder on my own words.

EPHEM: Inside my Fishing House I installed a beaufet with folding doors empanelled with a holy triptych – images of myself and Piscator flanking my young muse – with portraits of trout and grayling and the *Royal Charles* underneath.

It was my goodly Simon who gave me his angle rod. In such virtuous acts, all good men share.

But oh I was left a terrible legacy. Although I inherited an extensive estate upon my father's demise, it was encumbered with lawsuits that I grappled with all my life.

In solace, I escaped abroad, wrote texts, pamphlets and poems and I translated the work of Michel de Montaigne from the French.

But only angling gave me complete freedom. When I had a rod in my hand, I was released and enraptured.

My noble ancestor Tom fought with Henry V at Agincourt and saved the king's life. My forebears ranked dukes and princes in filial bonds … and me! I was left a poisoned cup and had to forfeit our thousand acres to retreat to London in misery, only the constancy of my own dear Piscator allaying my doom.

PEDES: Your angst has been a long time in its fermenting.

But enough of this regret Ephemator! We'll live in this moment for this moment is all we have.

The good was not interred with your bones and it flowers now to out shine the rank weeds. Remember your excellent book *The Compleat Gamester* and your stirring and musical poems? We'll take their perpetual seeds and raise a whole hillside of blooms. This is our mission for the poems you wrote still petal the shelves and hear this – forever you're known as *The Father of Fly Fishers* – The Fly Fishers Club paid for the installation of your plaque in St James's Church – and some of your fly dressings are still used.

Why, only last month in a pool just below Viator's Bridge in Mill Dale, I caught a fine trout using your own pattern. Do you remember the instructions you gave for tying the blue dun? I had great fun finding a black greyhound and combing its neck to tease out the hairs you described as the finest blue you ever saw.

PISC: Yes, you've left much to the world. Pedestrian speaks well. Desist. No further bleak utterance must pass your lips.

And truly my lips are dry.

Attendant, if I may trouble you for another bottle of your sparkling wine, we'd share another glass with this equally splendid pie.

Thank you sir.

Now take this singular coin in payment. No earthly mint ever produced laurelled heads like those.

Keep it in memory of a golden night.

SECOND DAY

CHAPTER ONE

Leg stretching

Monday. The Feast of St Ulric. Early Morning. Tottenham High Cross, Tottenham High Road, London.

PEDES: We'll begin our pilgrimage on foot at this ancient High Cross. You'll remember it, dating as it does from the 17th century. Since weathered, corrupted, damaged and repaired in 1809 by local residents, it still draws the spirit for momentary reflection midst a sea of noise and fumes. It's a fitting milestone for the proper start of our journey to the River Lea.

From here, we'll turn east through a maze of modern highways that have long replaced the countryside of your time. And here, I hesitate gentlemen.

Perhaps we should take a further taxi to avoid walking on these busy roads?

Having reconnoitred our route from here to our final destination in Hartington, I have to divulge that the vast changes you'll witness over the next few miles give me some concern. The impact of modern man has swamped this area in a constriction of roads, factories, housing estates, power stations and looming lines of electricity pylons. You'll see an array of the power lines I speak of over there.

For many years the Lea and its tributaries have been the drinking fountain of the metropolis and have been constrained and vastly manipulated to the needs of man.
In decades past, straight channels were dug, the diverted waters carrying floating craft ladened with all manner of goods for London town. That traffic has now ceased to be replaced by pleasure craft and a new era has dawned, the vital and ever purer Lea still laving and nourishing a new generation, some of its quieter arms and backwaters becoming protected havens for wild birds and flowers and yes, for your once detested otters.

However, only recognisable trickles of the old streams remain to retreat and cower like brutalised children, shunning all noise and clamour. Thirteen vast reservoirs now impound the waters of the Lea, Stort and Ash supplying the capital with 10% of its needs and although cargoes no longer continue to be carried on the intersecting network of canals, the legacies of the vast undertakings that rearranged more good earth hereabouts than the construction of any Egyptian pyramid, are still with us.

I'm a blunt Tyke gentlemen … so I have to say it. You'll see things as we head north from here that might make your whiskers curl. Although I love this area and applaud its continuing transformation, I tug at my own beard sometimes, particularly abhorring the drinks cans, the mounds of litter and the abandoned supermarket trolleys and I shudder at imagining your own reactions.

Brace yourselves. If you weren't on temporary leave of absence from your graves, you might turn in them!

PISC: Steady yourself my friend and dampen your concerns for us. You've previously indicated that much is being done to remedy the exploitations of old, so let us be content with that. Anything we see in the course of our onward journey to offend our eyes will strengthen our resolve and we'll be informed by it. Negative sights will serve only to nurture the flowers of renewal and nothing will disturb us. Let such thoughts stoke our endeavours.

And no, we'll not recall the taxi. We'll walk from here.

PEDES: We're now leaving the traffic behind and we enter, with a collective sigh of relief, the Lee Valley Regional Park and the Tottenham Marshes, the largest public open space in the area.

Can you feel the draw of your old stream Piscator? Like a primeval grazer can you sniff the familiar odour on the breeze?

My step quickens.

There! A glint of quicksilver.

Off I go again in giddy appreciation. Pardon me gentlemen.

But my! Water is so fundamental to life isn't it? Water is life! Wouldn't you both agree?

The Lea has been diverted and its character vastly changed down the centuries but it lives!

And isn't it amazing to think that its atoms are eternal, sustaining generation after generation of men like us in a virtuous cycle?

Why, the same sprinklings that cooled your neck in 1653 will fill my tankard this night.

I do hope you both washed behind your ears!

PISC: Please Pedestrian. Do slow down. We cannot match your pace. Your long years on the hills have girthed your sinews but our age and the atrophy of rest doth brake our perambulations.

But we were warned … weren't we Ephemator?

EPHEM: I affirm that caution Piscator, a winged messenger informing me that the velocity of Pedestrian's stride had caused his children to groan and whimper and to repeat an oft used complaint: 'Are we nearly there dad? You promised it was just over the next hill a whole mountain range back'.

And I was told that one of your walking companions famously groaned – 'A Markham mile is a mile and a bit and nobody exactly knows of what the bit consists'.

PEDES: A thousand pardons gentlemen. I'll slow down by this Stonebridge Lock.

But can't you recall the first time you ever saw a fabled brook? Didn't you rush to its banks all aquiver, scattering cows, raising flocks of birds and flattening flowers, making so much commotion at the edge that every terrified fish for a thousand yards splashed and fled as if pursued by a flock of demented gannets? And did it matter not, such was the impossibility of threading a line through the eye of a hook that shook and vibrated like a weathercock in a gale?

PISC: Yes, I can remember the first time I saw my own stream and thank you for reminding me of those honeyed moments.

Recollection is so sweet.

Your passion is infectious Sir. But how is excitement such as yours maintained through adolescence and manhood and through blank days and droughts and deluge? Your sovereign answer must surely enrich your book as well as any wisdom of ours?

PEDES: Dear friends, in rare but treasured moments, I'm splashed with charismatic drops and spy the universe in a grain of sand, every molecule orbiting to harmony and perfection. When that window of enlightenment fully opens – and I must polish the glass each day – I realise that our destiny and purpose is not so much the brotherhood of man but more a fellowship of particles, each mirroring itself, every reflection diminishing separation to the vanishing point of one mind, the mind of God.

When the blessing is upon me I have the gift of perennially seeing the universe thorough the eyes of an unsullied, ego-liberated child. At those times, from the droplet to the ocean, there's wonder in most everything I see, the energy of a realm beyond senses fuelling the joy of connectivity and inclusiveness.

Yes, you could say I really enjoy my angling … and so much more.

PISC: You're words are as invigorating as this early morning dew.

Look how it kicks up a rainbow shower!

Come on. Keep up! I'm sprinting now!

EPHEM: Stop Master! Might we tarry here by this bridge?

PEDES: What! Tired already? We've gone but a few yards.

EPHEM: No, gentle guide. My limbs are ready and strained. 'Tis a wafting indulgence, a craving that arrests me.

Pray stop for a moment while I produce a wand that casts a beguiling spell that has endured these three centuries. Redundant neath my cloak, reviled and resisted by the heavenly key holders, it once fumed in terrible fire, from volcanic rock carved and transformed into a votive bowl for the most compulsive burning.

See. Here, my pipe!

I hope the tobacco in this leathern pouch and my vestas have lasted as well?

Glory be! A spark and the ignition. Now silent both as I close my eyes and draw the ambrosial smoke.

PISC: Those tell-tale coils ascend to heaven and could delay your re-ascent by another three hundred years. I'll fetch a pail and we'll pray for forgiveness together, offering a jolly line to speed the absolution.

Tell me Ephemator, why smoke a haddock when you could have a pipefish and a mild sea-gar?

EPHEM: Very droll. Very droll indeed. But just one more puff before we go.

PEDES: Come along Vesuvius and quench those sparks. And yes, those eruptions make me think.

Tell us Ephemator ... weren't you shopping for bread in the Pudding Lane bake house of Mr Thomas Farynor on the 2nd September 1666?

Admit it Sir! It was your smoking that caused the Great Fire of London wasn't it?

PISC: Here is the reclusive stretch of the original River Lea Pedestrian promised us. I'm reminded of the words I quoted of an ingenious Spaniard in the opening pages of our book: '... rivers and the inhabitants of the watery element were made for wise men to contemplate and fools to pass by without consideration'.

PEDES: Such wisdom defies the years.

In my own time, Bernard Venables the author of *Mr Crabtree Goes Fishing* – it was one of favourite books as a boy – similarly remarked: 'I make a very close link between our belonging here and the will to fish. There is no natural medium in which the sense of life on Earth is more evident than in water ... most things which are least pleasant about life now are things which are most antithetical to fishing'.

It seems that our sport like no other brings out the philosopher in man.

It's now known that all life originated in the sea and we have an affinity with water. It's the most essential ingredient in the make up of our planet that ensures life.

To love fishing is to love life.

EPHEM: I found fishing a sovereign diversion and an escape – especially from fellows who were hounding me for money! I could lose myself with my line and angle and I was very hard to find especially when I could bolt into my favourite cave!

PEDES: Your cave indeed! The hideaway has still some notoriety and we'll pass it on the way.

PISC: I think one of the best foundations for being at one with the world is to love all nature, to love God and a special woman.

As you may know, I was a devout Christian and I enjoyed the friendship of many clergy and bishops. I was also blissfully married.

Your relationship with the universe can radiate from such twin loves. When you love, you love everything and everything you touch is gilded. Love is radiant. The love of God and a good woman is purest diamond. It attracts your life light and scatters it in a thousand directions and you yourself become that finest crystal. Drawing down such energy infused my angling with a reverence. And, as you so eloquently recounted yesterday dear Pedestrian when you spoke of your mystical encounter with a salmon under the Seven Sister Cliffs in Sussex, any excursion to the riverbank was also for me akin to entering the holiest cathedral.

PEDES: I too call myself a Christian and I'm also married to a very special woman and I've experienced such a mingling. Your ego melts in such radiance and you become one – the observer is the observed – this blissful state allowing you to become a true disciple of the angle where you may lose your identity at the bank to meld with the flow and become as seamless as its rush and ripple.

EPHEM: Such insights go way beyond ordinary comprehension gentlemen. I'm a poet fevered to dip his inkwell on the rush of senses.

PISC: Be reassured my adopted son. The universe appears as a conundrum of confusion but behind all the apparent complexity reigns a simplicity fuelled by a mind that eternally gravitates to order, concord and symmetry.

Take yourself brook side as a thoughtless and carefree child to those hallowed banks where the golden shafts of mind are focused brightest. Go there and feel a surging oneness, a oneness that need not be understood or analysed.

Let's go there, we three.

Come, link arms as brothers. We continue north along this path together.

PEDES: Here we are at Pickett's Lock Master, its notice board uplifting the spirits in rejoicing at the abundance of local wildlife. The list includes an animal that, I have to say, you once decried. The poor creature that brought forth your judgement that all keepers of hounds ought to have pensions from the king to encourage them to destroy the breed was, by my own time, almost extinct. However, the law now protects the beast and enlightened attitudes prevail, anglers and those whiskered fish-eaters hunting side by side. Three cheers for the otter!

I'm sure Sir, given the totally different circumstances of these modern times that you'd have been willing to share your catch? After all, in the grand scheme of things, isn't newcomer man the poacher? And wasn't the beautiful otter angling for trout while we were foraging for roots and berries?

PISC: Indeed, I accept the conclusion of long perspective as rightful censure of a man boasting green credentials. I answer for my bellicosity with contrition and I crave the forgiveness of generations of anglers – and otters! – dear Pedestrian. The vehemence of my assault on the beast is not befitting of my claim that angling is somewhat like poetry. My unkind and ill-measured words have struck a discordant note and have disturbed my celestial rest. They're unmelodic and disharmonious and I strike them out, substituting new paragraphs for the umpteenth reprinting! If nothing else, this adventure fosters a recantation and I'm grateful for that.

Now what's this?

My old boughs have been replaced by a thicket of angle rods and I spy a veritable cohort of anglers spaced as equidistant pawns on a chessboard, each man sitting on a cushioned box at numbered marks.

Tell me what manner of sport is this?

PEDES: This congregation of silent Buddha's is known as a fishing match, each contestant waging coin on the heaviest net to claim the prize.

EPHEM: The fish are not to larders bound?

PEDES: No. When whistles blow, the match is done and men with weighing scales decide the day. All fish are then restored to live and breed for a grand repeating.

In youth, I often joined such bands, just the mention of Cowthorpe on my own River Nidd making my heart flutter. Why, it was there one cold September day that I wrestled with a fish that won me a king's ransom, a silvered bream delivering a chest of gold!

EPHEM: These endeavours appeal to my sporting nature, combining angling and the thrills of the green baize.

Excuse me Sir – you at Number 41 – pray tell us what you've caught?

ANGLER 41: I suppose it's a form of praying but it don't seem to be doing me a lot o' good. I've caught bugger all.
PISC: Perhaps it's the appearance of your heavy float that disturbs the fish my friend? The splash is most disruptive.

ANGLER 41: It's not the appearance I'm bothered about governor. I'm more interested in its disappearance.

But what do old geezers like you know about fishing anyway?

PEDES: I'll surprise you Sir.

Go along you two. I'll catch you up.

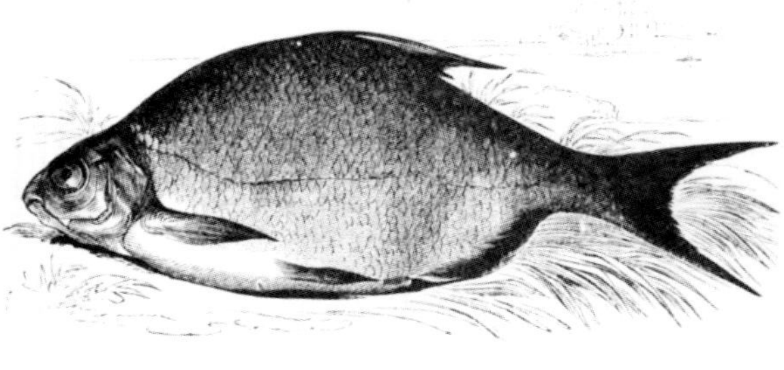

PISC: There you are Pedestrian. You overtake us.

Oh how I'm relishing this hearty stroll, our comrade talk gobbling up the yards unseen.

As you've said, since the dawn of time this mode of interacting with the world has been ordained as man's best way of modulating with the very heartbeats of life.

And I feel that we three are really getting to know each other.

PEDES: I feel that too Piscator and I'm loving this day.

But I'm curious. Tell me about your relationship with Ephemator and how you two first became acquainted. The history books are largely silent on the matter.
PISC: As you know, I'm a great deal older than our dear friend. I'm a man of ninety years. How old are you Ephemator? Remind me.

EPHEM: I'm fifty-six. I was a young man when I first met you. You came to Beresford Hall as a guest of my father's. Remember our first meeting?

PISC: I recall it with great clarity. I can't fix a date but I know the stains on my shirt were ever obdurate to the washing. Burgundy wine has such deep tones.

Your father was a man of great learning and was a fine scholar and writer even if he was a little dissolute with money. We had many mutual friends. We met that summer's day in the library and discoursed on many things. You burst in with imprecations and a bottle to your lips.

I didn't mind the drowning but was embarrassed for my host and those poor damp books.

The man before us Pedestrian was quarrelsome as a boy and was something of a firebrand but the angle rod and the tutorings of young Simon helped temper him.

EPHEM: Transpose just two letters Master! Ang-e-l. You were my angel!

After the death of my friend and dear mother, you took me gently down to Dove side and bade me sit in contemplation as you cast a line and bathed my brow with oil and sweet herbs.

As were peered, you talked long and passionately about God's bounty and the richness of life, your soothing mellow voice coaxing me to torpor.

Afterwards, during the following week when I recovered some pallor to my cheeks, we put aside your primitive corks and leaden drams and I demonstrated the guile of fly-fishing – you impaled a lamb! T'was no wonder you commissioned those later chapters in your fifth edition!

From despair to divinity in one redeeming week!

No, I never forgot those first meetings with Mr Izaak Walton.

You dear Sir were my direction and afterwards, you encouraged all that was good in my life. You taught me respect and drew out the poet in me. The compass needle constantly wavered but near or far your guiding presence was always with me and I'll announce it again this second day, as I'll proclaim it these seven days and forever more – Oh Master – I love you!

PEDES: Before you two begin to overflow the Lee Navigation with your tears, we'll sit on this bench and enjoy a flask of tea.

EPHEM: It's so hot!

PEDES: Sip it slowly.

For our refreshment, I would have brought you to the Bleak Hall mentioned in your book but it's been absorbed as old bones somewhere in this scene. Your pages reek with the odours of its pungent ale and clean lavender-strewn sheets but the old abode is no more.

I'm confused but this surely was the site of the ancient Cook's Ferry?

A portion of the inn remained somewhere here until recent times, consisting of a kitchen with a room above ascended by an outside staircase. For some years it lingered on in ruination and was called by our fraternity the 'Fishermen's Locker' where tackle and the paraphernalia of the match fishermen were kept. Now it's no more.

PISC: It's surely gone from view but harken to a deeper reality.

Like 41's float, nothing really disappears.

Every wholesome thought or action is imprinted in the eternal matrix to resonate forever. If you would become a sounding board, you can feel the good vibrations here and everywhere.

Linger and absorb the benevolence of this special place.

Suspend all thinking and allow the past to seep and wander.

Despite the pressing city throng, I feel the thrill of moments past when this was but nature's garden where I caught a fat chub. And it's still a garden!
The remembrance in our book comes bubbling to my lips like an infant spring:

Look! under that broad beech tree I sat down when I was last this way a-fishing. And the birds in the adjoining grove seemed to have a friendly contention with an echo, whose dead voice seemed to live in a hollow tree, near to the brow of that primrose hill. There I sat viewing the silver streams glide silently towards their centre; the tempestuous sea; yet sometimes opposed by rugged roots and pebble-stones, which broke their waves and turned them into foam. And sometimes I beguiled time by viewing the harmless lambs; some leaping securely in cool shade, whilst others sported themselves in the cheerful sun; and saw others craving comfort from the swollen udders of bleating dams. And I thus sat, these and other sights has so fully possessed my soul with content, that I thought, as the poet hath happily expressed it,

I was for that time lifted above the earth,
And possessed of joys not promised in my birth.

EPHEM: They're two fine lines worthy of my muse's pen.

PISC: But there's more!

As I left this place, and entered into the next field, a second pleasure entertained me: 'twas a handsome milkmaid with her milkmaid mother -.

EPHEM: I so adored the milkmaids!

PISC: – '*twas a handsome milkmaid, that had not yet attained so much age and wisdom as to load her mind with any fears of many things that will never be –*

PEDES: She lived in the moment!

PISC: – *that will never be (as too many men too often do); but she cast away all care and sung like a nightingale.*

Look yonder! I wrote this and more. *On my word, yonder they both be a-milking again. I'll give them the chub and persuade them to sing songs.*

God speed you good woman! I've been a-fishing and I'm going to Bleak Hall to my bed and having caught a chub I'll bestow it upon you and your daughter

The milkmaids thanked me and promised to brew a syllabub of new verjuice for my next visit, saying that they loved all anglers as honest, civil and quiet men.

And before our parting they gave me a draught of red cows milk and sang their songs:

The silver dishes for thy meat,
As precious as the gods do eat,
Shall, on an ivory table be,
Prepared each day for thee and me.

EPHEM: Ye gods! The heavenly kings would retch on such meat. Chub? It's the vilest meat that swims.

PEDES: It makes the pike I spoke of yesterday taste like ambrosia.

I've heard tell that chub flesh is similar to a dish of darning needles and sour wool.

PISC: Yes, see your animation! The convivial chords that once lilted here are echoed still. I hear the legacy of laughter and the sweet refrains and drain a full tankard of Bleak Hall brew.

EPHEM: Drink your tea.

PEDES: This is Enfield Dock hard by Enfield Island Village. The village is perennially identified with guns. They were manufactured here in there thousands and transported to London by barge, the Lee Enfield rifle making the hamlet famous. Thankfully, the boring machines have gone and the only reminder of Enfield's explosive past is in the name of the Gunpowder Park just a few hundred yards to the east.

Frankly though, I don't like guns.

Let's resist calling in at the *Greyhound* to wet our whistles and press on to Ramney Marsh and another icon of this technological age.

EPHEM: What would that be Pedestrian?

PEDES: We'll shortly come to a major highway called the M25. It circles the entire London metropolis carrying millions of vehicles every week. They swirl around the compass in never-ending spirals like distant nebulae creating thunderous winds of noise, vibration and ghastly fumes.

As you may have gathered, I'm not too fond of the M25 either.

PISC: Harken. Is that the sound of the highway now?

PEDES: It is Master. It'll get progressively louder as we get nearer to the span across the water. We need to lengthen our strides and put this place behind us as quickly as we can.

But Good Lord! Would you look at that?

If my cheeks were burning at Tottenham High Cross, they're positively molten now.

I'm ashamed and embarrassed to have led you both here to witness the despoliation of your once green banks. The milkmaids have long gone.

Have you ever seen such degeneration?

There, under the flyover. See the utter squalor competing with the roar and pollution above – the soiled mattresses and rusted chairs, the still smouldering campfires and the mounds of rotten food and rubbish pecked over by flocks of magpies. It's a scene from hell. It must be a nightly refuge for the poor and unfortunate down and outs of London who no doubt will return in a few short hours.

But what do you make of that even more extraordinary sight?

Over there at the water's edge. Do you see them? They're both seated – a fisherman and his wife – oblivious to the shambles behind and the cacophony above.

My God! He's transfixed to his float and she's absorbed in the pages of a book!

I'd rather angle in the Styx!

Sorry gentlemen.

PISC: You need not apologise Pedestrian. Rather you should look again in deep reflection.

You spoke of this place as an icon. Indeed it is. But rather than recoiling at the sight you should embrace it.

PEDES: What?

PISC: Open your eyes my friend. The couple are in deep abstraction. They're only yards from the detritus of a sometimes ugly world but they're transported to a greener realm.

I simply ask, what better endorsement could there be for the contemplative man's recreation?

I need say no more save this. This one moment on the first day of our odyssey can define our whole mission.

Thank you for leading us here Pedestrian.

PEDES: This, you'll be glad to know, is as far as we go today gentlemen. We've reached the outskirts of Waltham Abbey nearby. Fragments of the old abbey remain but we've not time to explore them today.

You've walked well. I do hope you've enjoyed our excursion?

You can relax for a hot bath awaits you.

What planning! Look! There! By the lane side. Our vehicle already awaits our convenience. It'll speed us in just five minutes to a mansion built to replace King James's palace referred to in your book.

Thanks cabbie for coming so soon.

Theobalds Park Hotel if you please.

SECOND DAY

CHAPTER TWO

The kingship of angling

Monday. The Feast of St Ulric. Evening. Theobalds Park Hotel, Waltham Cross.

PISC: Pardon me if I totter just a little stiffly to my chair gentlemen. I've spent so much time a-seated listening to harps and heavenly choirs that my joints are creaked.

But urged on by your tales of that Yorkshire Methuselah Henry Jenkins, I accomplished much today and have savoured each furlong.

I'm a nonagenarian but compared to him, I'm but a pap-fast babe.

PEDES: My! Yes, what a man! A contemporary of yours, he lived through the reigns of eight monarchs ascribing his longevity to good old Yorkshire ale – the famous Stingo – Wensleydale Cheese and walking.

I've generously partaken of both foods throughout my life and have always used my legs for their divine purpose.

I wonder? If I keep striding out, do you think I'll live to 169?

PISC: I'm sure of it Sir!

Walking is your abiding love and what you love sustains you … even to sixteen score years and nine!

You'll be a fabled walker yet and we needed such a man for the task upon us.

You'll not realise this – and again I risk a censure in the rash divulging – but you were chosen to lead Ephemator and I on this reprising tour.

Are you surprised?

We needed a man – both an angler and a walker – who could draw out the best in us and refresh our book in a modern rendering, nudging the helms of your readers to calmer waters.

And we needed a man who could accept a well-meant reproach.

Your reaction was admirable back there.

I know you'll not feel demeaned by this, but in present times there are legions of men who eclipse your skill with rod and line and who've trod the greater distance. But for our sacred purpose we coveted simple passion more, your empathy with the world and your great joy at the resounding munificence of life singling you out from a whole host of other candidates, your beloved wife Lora giving you a superb reference and that patron saint of the American wilderness, John Muir also.

I can tell you that a convocation of noble feet, we amongst them, was convened aloft, Henry Jenkins presiding.

Around the table were some of your favourite Yorkshiremen, Canon Arthur Neville Cooper, Foster Powell and Alfred J Brown together with Muir, George Borrow, Samuel Taylor Coleridge, Captain Barclay, Carl Philipp Moritz, Hilaire Belloc and Robert Louis Stevenson.

I know you've devoured all their books and were particularly inspired by Muir and Cooper who you once described as a rustic Socrates.

Can you remember referring to his clarion call to legs that had the pull of a spring tide?

He told me you'd often quoted from his books *Quaint Talks About Long Walks, The Tramps of the Walking Parson, A Tramp's Schooling* and *Round the Home of a Yorkshire Parson* and that you were most fond of his special lines:

The man who walks is the man who is well.

Everywhere there is a desire to return to a natural life, for it is evident from the health of the nation that something has gone wrong. The ancient philosophers who sought the Elixir of Life failed in their search because they looked in every direction but the right one ... it lies in the deep draughts of oxygen one drinks in from the air around us.

And lastly:

I covet the never-ending relish that toil imparts.

PEDES: I'm amazed and humbled Master. What did these holy men conclude?

PISC: That from the entire world, you were the man for the job, the parson himself suggesting the artifice with the talking chimney.

And one last thing. On successful completion of your mission, you are promised an undisclosed miracle.

So here we are!

PEDES: It's the honour of a lifetime and I'm so pleased to be here to guide you.

EPHEM: The honour is all ours Pedestrian. Pedestrian. It's a royal title better than any plumes and fancies.

PEDES: I hope I wear it well.

So, sit you both and take a quenching sip of champagne for we celebrate this night.

EPHEM: What do we celebrate Pedestrian?

PEDES: We celebrate my divine appointment.

We rejoice at our trinity of men.

We salute the glassmaker who with hot breath made this crystalled bottle. We raise a fanfare of bugles for the people who produced the wine within to give us such luscious drink. We ring bells in praise of the blessed oak that bequeathed its bark to seal our nectar fresh. We applaud the label maker who with a flick of artful wrist has conjured a bucolic scene to salivate the senses. And we pay great respects to our waiter, who with the deftest twist and tug has released a trillion excited bubbles to the world.

We celebrate our triple journey.

Raise your goblets.

We celebrate life gentlemen.

Cheers!

Now take the menu. You must choose this night.

PISC: Had it been offered, I would have chosen the highly esteemed bream. But no matter.

I suppose, as one of the world's most feted piscivores, I should have fish again?

Yes, I'll have the salmon.

What's your choice my friends?

EPHEM/PEDES: I also choose the salmon.

EPHEM: We echo in tandem Pedestrian. Most apt, for in reclining before this feast I did again cast a fly into your little book, my *Royal Charles* raising your poem *The Leaper*.

May I recite it Master? I have the book here.

PISC: I'd be delighted to hear it as we drink our cauliflower soup.

PEDES: You do me a second great honour Sir.

EPHEM: I hope my gravelled tones do it justice.

The Leaper

Morgue slapped.
Displayed, the bounty of the sea arranged in labelled ranks.
Lifeless corpses, disembowelled, bulge-eyed, last gasps echoing in contorted funeral masks.

Examine heads that butted a thousand tides.
Finger iridescent flanks that braved the aquamarine and grow sombre.

On that silver dish, prized amongst the fallen … a salmon.
Plucked in the full torrent of life.
Rendered up, butchered, Salome's repugnant gift, the saddest meat of all.

And yet…

Brave warrior caste.
War cries!

To the colours! Salmo salar!
Effulgent rod, St Elmo fired.
Laurelled fish! Rise up!

And there's a little addendum note at the foot.

Recalling a near blank day on the River Tweed at Coldstream in Scotland, a salmon leaping in the gloaming, snatching a Thunder and Lightning and leading this poet on a merry dance. The fish was returned unharmed.

PISC: I think I'll prevaricate and order a lamb chop.

It's a wonderfully visceral tribute to the plight of our noblest fish Pedestrian. You have real respect for the beast.

PEDES: I have Master. And the taste…!

And here comes our platter decorated with parsley and lemon.

But before you gather your knives and forks, allow me to impart a detail that will aid your digestion.

The fish before us never braved that aquamarine for it was farmed.

Yes, it was raised as sheep and cattle, the pastures of deep Scottish lochs producing such a bounty of salmon that this former dish of kings is now as cheap as the day a barrel load of your herrings were sold for a farthing piece.

You can tuck in gentlemen knowing that the wild *salmo salar* swims protected and free.

EPHEM: It's most toothsome Pedestrian, the potatoes and asparagus serving as the perfect companions.

Truly, we do dine like the kings who once lived in Theobalds Palace.

PEDES: Then let's talk of kingship – the kingship of angling.

Tell me Ephemator about your favourite mode of angling.

Tell me about fly-fishing. Why do you favour it so?

EPHEM: Well, firstly, it's what my good Simon taught me. Every time I grasped his rod at my own Dove bank, I drifted in happy memory. I ventured not to his absent mound but sought out his streamside spirit, finding it there with each cast and flick.

He left not only snagged and tangled flies on the pinnacle of rock that was his true tombstone. Etched in a more timeless stone, he left me a friendship that in times of considerable trouble during my life, drew me back time and again to that spot where we first fished.

I took up his angle rod as a bishop raising his spangled crozier, the raising becoming benediction and blessing.

Sometimes hounded and insulted, I retreated to the bank and found a balm to tears and trouble, the rhythms of my casting plunging me carefree and untroubled into the motions of infinity that, like my looping figures of eight, had no beginnings and shall have no end.

I fly-fished at first in memory of my dear friend but I found the method most suited to my often fevered and reckless temperament, the constant movement of rod and line and the hawk-eye blinkings for betraying swirls and dimples, demanding a concentration that dissolved all woe.

Compared to the preferences of my Master who languuored with floats and leads and wiggly worms, mine is the supreme form of angling.

Fly-fishing is the best!

PEDES: What say you to such upstart talk Piscator?

PISC: Tirade and outrageous calumny!

'Tis true I was never in concord with so much wafting and waving. And the intricacies of weaving spiders' webs to inveigh the trout were far too taxing for dim eyes.

Ephemator has the sap of aspen in his blood. There's a summer cordial of rose and elder flowers in mine, more suited to my slow and tender ways.

Particularly in my vintage years, I eschewed the ecstasies of mountain brooks where plungeth youthful feet in rush and tumble, seeking out meadows where I could sit upon a tuffet dry shod under a shaded arbour of honeysuckle to dream, bee-buzz, distant calls of larks and linnets and the rhythmic swish of harvest scythes coaxing me to lethargy and sometimes, I admit, to slumber.

At those times, even in those times when St George fled from dragons breath and battled with himself, I went to my meanderings and with pen and crisp parchment, I wrote these words. They're imprinted on my soul:

No life is so happy and so pleasant as the life of a well-governed angler, for when the lawyer is swallowed up with business, and the statesman is preventing or contriving plots, then we sit on cowslip banks, hear the birds sing and possess ourselves in as much quietness as these silent silver streams we now see glide so quietly by. God never did make a more calm, quiet, innocent recreation than angling.

I scribbled those lines just a few days after the carnage at Marston Moor. But alas, the perpetrators were traitors not statesmen.

But I vacillate and wander like my favourite stream.

In certainty, my angling meat was of a less lusty kind and 't'was no matter what the quarry.

My animated friend dashed about his brook as Aeolus with wings but my preference was for a more sedentary craft, static sweetmeats plunged with leads and clever wires luring not just trout and grayling but anything that swam.

And I was much more catholic in my sport, esteeming all fish regardless of their kind.

How I adored gazing into the eyes of summer rudd, their upturned lips puckered as for a kiss!

And my big-mouthed perch – her gap could not out-gape my spouse's mother's hole! nor so her dorsal spikes to sting! But she was gorgeous in her stripes of black and golden green.

Next in my fishy cavalcade that doctor fish, the tench, her bubbled calling cards announcing hot day dawns. Solid as that in-laws chubby thighs – forgive me sweet Celeste I jest! she cruised the muddy depths to find the bait, my knobbed paste of bread and honey she caressing.

What of the muscled barbel that hugged the streamy bed? My angle rod was oft in arcs and splinters afore he showed his head.

My goodness! How my words sparkle this evening. What's in this wine that beguiles me to such frivolity and verse Pedestrian?

Here waiter if you please. A second bottle while the muse attends me.

PEDES: It's not the champagne Master but the company that coaxes your lyricism.

Pray do continue.

Ephemator and I are enjoying your company like no other.

PISC: In my litany, I must include the wrapping eel, a beast of woeful deprecation. Fashioned as a serpent, he's long endured an undeserved comparison with Old Nick's writher, his pluck and determination in voyaging from distant seas – I'm thrilled that you've banished the mystery Pedestrian – to ascend our rivers and there to spawn and prosper even excelling the courage of this salmon.

Have you ever tried the jellied eels that were in my time so popular in these parts? Most delicious.

From my list, I cannot omit the chub. You've chuckled ribald words at my fondness for the fish but I do admire him. In a silvered waistcoat, he cruises the stream like some fat alderman at my Lord Mayor's luncheon, his monocled eye spying tit-bits to taste and nibble. I liked to catch him best with a natural fly procured from a copse or thicket, impaling the creature on a weighted hook and creeping, with a short line wound around my angle rod, to an overhanging bough for clandestine deployment.

Solicitous of betraying creaks and shadows, I would cautiously inch along the branch to unwind and drop my fly towards an unsuspecting fish.

And gr-ad-ual-ly, with my heart pounding and my knees wobbling, I would poke my rod from beyond the furthest leaf and let the line drop towards the surface, steering the insect towards the inquiring nose.

Then like the alderman who could not resist the last free savoury pie, he'd rise and gobble, sometimes pulling me off my perch to join him!

But what of your angling preferences Pedestrian?

You've heard from we both.

Now entertain us with your stories.

PEDES: Well gentlemen, I can say I've fished in every water and with every method in rivers, lakes and salt, and by far my best pleasure is derived from deploying the trotting float in rivers using a technique known as fine and far off. I was almost born to it.

But let me start at the beginning.

I was a poor scholar.

In school day dreams I was distracted from my books, even flying missiles from the accurate hand of Chalky White not rousing me to learn. Staring out of the window as that exasperated teacher poked me with a stick, I'd no interest in algebra, geography or the triumphs of ancient Rome, thoughts of a finned morsel swallowing me whole.

On those boring Wednesday afternoons, my lessons would drone on by, me urging the hands of the classroom clock to sprint to the magical three o' the hour when a motorcar would arrive at the school gates to whisk me to paradise.

I was collected by a family friend Charlie who was a traveller in the Leeds clothing trade, he always contriving a countryside appointment with a client upon that appointed day.

We travelled to Kirk Hammerton on the Nidd, the tone of our engine seeming to get ever quieter as we threaded the country lanes that led to a village where we turned off by a Saxon church and on down a cart track to a derelict mill by the river.

Its water wheel was silent and cobwebbed and three teetering floors cracked and creaked with age, chattering swallows flitting from its sagging eaves and windows. Below was a swirling weir and nearby, in a side channel, a sunken barge.

Hurrying through a gate, we waded chest high through summer flowers to the water where I was left under a willow tree to fumble.

I've all ready told you how my fingers so trembled with anticipation at the prospect of fishing that I found it difficult to tie a hook.

Well it wasn't just my fingers that shook.

My whole body was a palsy of expectation, every corpuscle and nerve fibre firing off like flashes of lightning.

The taking up of an angle rod was all the excitements of life in one confection.

It was my first communion and my first kiss.

It was my first and only goal for St Patrick's Football Club.

And it was my first dam burst experience of physical love.

PISC: Oh! Memories! We can both relate to that can't we Ephemator?

Sorry Pedestrian … do carry on.

PEDES: Well, I was shaking so much that sometimes, when assembling my rod, I'd fail to line up the rod rings properly. I'd only loosely fix the reel. It would fall off into a cow pat or into the water. And when I'd retrieved it, cleaned it and begun to thread the line, I'd miss out a rod ring.

Then I'd snatch a porcupine quill float from my toffee tin and break its rubber-fixing ring. I'd get another and reach for a box of lead shot, spilling half its contents in the grass.

That helpful Mr Crabtree recommended that you carefully select the size of shot and arrange their patterns on the line to regulate sinking rates. And he knew that each float needed a precise amount of lead to ensure its cocking.

But I'd no time for all that!

I snatched away again, taking up the shot, any shot, in my fingers, using my teeth to bite onto the splits and fix the shot in any random position on the line. And I swallowed lots of lead.

I wont tell you how I retrieved it.

Not now.

Not when you're eating!

Then I got my hook and, holding it between my fingers with my arms firmly pushed against two branches to stop the shaking, I would pierce its eye … or my finger.

The line required knotting, Mr Crabtree going to great lengths in both words and pictures to explain the different types of knots and their applications.

But I'd no time for all that!

I tied my hook as I tied my shoelaces and they never came undone!

Finally came the bait and I reached into my hot and pungent bag to select a maggot.

In impaling the beast, Mr Crabtree gave instructions that you should study its anatomy, squeezing its body at one end, causing a protuberance of skin to appear. This flap was to be the impaling point, a careful hooking ensuring that no body fluids were leaked and that the maggot gave maximum wriggles.

But I'd no time for all that!

I plunged in like a frenzied swordsman stabbing the maggot midriff, sending tiny showers of its life force all over my fingers, the flaccid, flabby gobbet of bait hardly moving.

Then all was done and I could go a-fishing!

Eyes wide and panting I tossed my line into the middle of the stream and took a deep breath.

The float. Can you see it Master? It's flat upon the surface just near that bed of weed.

My quill. It has life. Do you catch it twitching Ephemator like Our Lord on that blessed Easter Day?

It's breaking from the surface film as bold as any May- blown fly and stands erect, a sentinel and symbol of the abundant fishy life below, sailing on, bobbing and dancing to glide, to dip, to prosper.

Look now both!

The float it plunges to hail a biting. And I strike and have him thrashing in all the exultancies of life.

Ring bells in yonder church and fill my cup again with more champagne for further celebration.

Sup deep. I've caught a bleak!

PISC: Ah the bleak. I wrote of that tiny fish in my book calling him the river swallow and the fresh-water sprat.

PEDES: In Yorkshire he's named the willow blade from his resemblance to a small leaf. But despite his diminutive size, he remains as one of my favourite fish, filling those Hammerton days with endless joy.

Indeed, his easy catching put all my fumbling ways to oblivion and I fished on those long summer Wednesday afternoons and evenings in total enchantment, shoals of silver bleak filling my creel like the mother load.

And as you again mentioned in your book, bleaks are very tasty.

EPHEM: But not, I wager, as tasty as this fat salmon?

PEDES: Quite so my friend. With your eyelids shut again, it's great to see you relishing your supper.

But let me conclude my narrative.

You never forget your first love and I never forgot my bleak and the manner of their capture, float fishing becoming my preferred method of angling.

I tried other techniques of course but found them lacking in involvement and animation.

Ledgering with heavy weights can deliver leviathan fish but personally, and pardon me Piscator, I found it a mighty yawn, the endless hours of peering at static tips having all the excitement of staring at a corpse.

A friend introduced me to spinning with flashy lures and spoons but I found all that thrusting and splashing disturbed both stream and concentration as did those herds of thirsty cows at their bankside drinking.

Later, I took up your fly rod Ephemator and I did enjoy the art particularly the casting with the dry fly, the rhythms and the visual elements of the sport appealing to my inclinations to absorption and engagement.

But I always came back to my floats, the craft of steering a searching buoy at many yards distant along deep glides, by rocks and those swirling places where my dipper bobbed and curtsied, being totally compelling.

But I've just remembered!

There was a tactic just recalled that excelled even this.

About two hundred yards below the mill was an old farm bridge ... it's all coming back to me now. Its span shaded a deep pool. There, on days when the sun shone bright, shoals of fish congregated to escape the heat, wraiths of silver-grey hovering between the piles.

Surface reflections usually clouded the depths but in certain lights when that bridge cast its deepest shadow, you could see the fish as in an aquarium, to approach unseen with neither float nor lead, a single maggot being the only sinker you'd need.

I went to that bridge with an old school friend, both of us creeping on bended knees to swish and dangle before their very snouts.

Angling could never have been more thrilling.

To see our quarry, to cast out a bait and to steer it close, watching spellbound as perch and dace and wary roach darted from their lairs for the snatching was wild adventure, two excited but exasperated boys eventually learning the trick of hooking the blessed things!

The secret was, to flick the hook in the instant before the fish *appeared* to mouth the bait. If you delayed until the fish was seen to swallow the bait, by the time the vision had been processed by the brain and instructions sent to the wrist to set the hook, the fish was gone!

This method we called pimping.

Short of diving in and grabbing the fish with my teeth like an otter, it was the most exciting method of angling I've ever tried.

I was taken to the Nidd most summer Wednesdays over several seasons, those carefree hours being some of the most precious in my boyhood.

When it became too dark to fish, Charlie had me reluctantly wind in and took me to the *Crown Inn* for refreshment. There, I stood tall, hoping that my small stature would not betray me as an under age drinker.

But my! I did enjoy that pint!

Afterwards, I'd be dropped off at the bottom of Bertha Street, Charlie pressing a three-penny piece in my hand to buy me a supper at Greenwood's Fish and Chip Shop. And there, leant against the window with a posse of street urchins about me stealing my chips and listening in awe, I'd brag about my adventures in that far off land, finally limping home dog-tired to dream until the following Wednesday.

Yes, I've only to say Kirk Hammerton and I swoon.

And I'll tell you this. If there's inferior enjoyment in heaven, you can count me out.

You can tell St Peter that if they don't serve a good pint of Tetley's up there … and a steaming 'one of each' – well he can forget it.

I'm staying put!

PISC: Ha! Just so. I'll have a word with him immediately upon our return … wont we Ephemator?

And we'll make sure he orders a whole barrel full of your Tetley's.

He'll maybe build a brewery?

Now, what shall we have to complete our feast my friends?

Please pass me the menu.

Oh. You shown me some strange and wonderful things these last two days dear Pedestrian and strangeness lurketh even here.

What's this spotted dick?

THIRD DAY

CHAPTER ONE

A-fishing!

Tuesday. The Feast of St Athanasius of Athos. Dawn. Theobalds Park Hotel, Waltham Cross.

PEDES: Wakey, wakey rise and shine, you broke your mother's heart, you wont break mine!

EPHEM: Argh! Someone assails the door and tests its hinges Master.

PISC: Aye, what banging is this? 'Tis enough to wake the dead.

EPHEM: But we are dead.

PISC: Well, yes, but not this week.

See who it is.

EPHEM: Oh! It's you Pedestrian.

You stand before me ready and booted.

Was it the surfeit of champagne that accounts for your early rising?

Or did you dampen your bed?

PEDES: No my friend. It's the Lazarus shafts that prised me up, the lance in the east poking me from sleep.

Come on! The day beckons and we're going a-fishing!

We'll meet you downstairs in fifteen minutes … wont we Piscator?

PISC: Huh?

PISC: Good morning Pedestrian … and thank your for your knocking and the laying out of fresh clothes and boots.

As you see, I've now dressed and risen although I know not whether I yet shine.

Yawn.

I'm feeling a little over-fortified this morn.

I'd forgotten that the brew imbibed in heaven is non-alcoholic.

PEDES: Please, take some of this fine coffee gentlemen. It'll sober and refresh you.

And do have some of these delicious croissants with crispy bacon and newly laid eggs.

EPHEM: Yet again Pedestrian you've laid a table to tempt the gods. The smell alone is enough to bring each night-capped guest rushing downstairs following his nose like a lodestone.

PEDES: Friends, pardon my knocking and my impudent alacrity. The excitement wells up inside me like the release of last night's nectar and I don't want to waste one second of this day.

The feeling I had as a child when my lovely mother scolded me for bolting my food as some ravenous wolf is still with me and I rejoice at it.

It's a gift.

I was then so keen to rejoin my playmates that, not tasting or seeing, I cleared my plate in a thrice. In a saying of the time, it never touched the sides!

It's as though, like some aboriginal man, my awakening from sleep and sense of heightened reality are so empirically fuelled as to merrily blaze.

But please, do take your time.

PISC: We will, wont we Ephemator?

I adore that smell Ephemator refers to but alas, all swine from our high place roam free and the only bacon I know is called Sir Francis.

He's a friend of mine.

I previously met the famous Lord Chancellor when I was about thirty years of age. We fished together for barbel at Richmond, afterwards discoursing at a riverside tavern on his scientific methods and on philosophy and logic.

And he confided something then that will astound you and all the readers of your book.

My, this bacon is good.

PEDES: What's that Master? I'm intrigued.

PISC: Brace your disbelieving self and know that he was indeed the author of all those plays ascribed to one William Shakespeare and chuckled at all the hot contentions and obfuscations that have beset academia for over three hundred years.

Before I left, he asked me, for once and for all, to put the matter straight and to tell you that William Shakespeare was the name he first gave to his cat!

Billy was a very talented feline!

EPHEM: Very interesting I'm sure but I'm eager to depart.

And here, apt to this instant, is one of my old poems:

Away then away,
We lose sport by delay,
But first leave all sorrows behind us.
If misfortune do come,
We are all gone from home,
And a-fishing she never can find us.

PEDES: Thanks cabbie for dropping us so close to the water.

Here, take this note and have a drink on us, toasting our bulging nets.

We're going a-fishing!

PISC: Just a little further along the bank gentlemen and we'll meet our man.

I'd originally intended to ask the manager of the *Theobalds Park Hotel* to organise our day's adventure but a chance meeting of yesterday was too fortuitous to ignore.

There he is, smiling and waving in expectation.

Good morning Angler 41!

We've a fine day for it! Why, even the bindweed weaves a magic spell on mornings like this.

May I introduce Mr Izaak Walton … and his friend and co-author Mr Charles Cotton.

ANGLER 41: Well, I never! I'm pleased to meet you both … again. I'm sorry about the wigging I gave you yesterday. I was right out of order. When this gentleman had a word in my shell-like I had a good laugh. I thought it was a wind up.

PISC:(Whispers) What is the man saying?

ANGLER 41: I'm a bit mutton Jeff see and had to ask him again. Izaak Walton and Charles Cotton I said. Weren't they the geezers that wrote that famous book on angling?

I didn't believe him o'course … not 'til he showed me the coin. Well, there was something about it that made me think. With the Big Chief's head on one side and St Peter's on the other it was a bit tasty. And when His Nibs blinked … well … stuff me with the blunt end of a ragman's trumpet! I knew then it must be true. It's a miracle!

Here, let me shake you both by the hand.

Wait 'til my missis hears about this. She'll throw a wobbler.

Now then. I got here early and everything's ready just as your friend asked. It's all pegged out and all four rigs are tackled up and waiting for the casts. And there's a bait box beside each fishing basket.

Will you make the draw Pedestrian?

PEDES: It would be my pleasure.

I'll fold the peg numbers.

Now, you see I wear the traditional flat cap. In time honoured fashion I'll spin it around on my pate until the peak is reversed, placing each folded ticket in a maggot bag, then licking my drawing finger at each dipping.

But before we draw, a recitation of the protocols.

You're fishing to the Lee Valley Country Park Rules. One rod and line only allowed and all anglers must use barbless hooks. All foul hooked fish to be returned immediately to the water. No hemp seed allowed. All other rules to be as here printed.

We'll fish between 8 o'clock and 10 o'clock, times to be adhered to on my shout.

And here's your sweeps – all prizes kindly donated by my publisher.

Winner-takes-all £100.

EPHEM: £100? I think I'll warm to this match fishing. Such a sum would have put every hound off my scent.

PEDES: Winner-takes-all £100. Largest fish £50. Most species £50.

Last man takes the scales.

Now for the draw gentlemen … and may the best man win.

PISC: Number 1. What's your fortune Ephemator?

EPHEM: I've plucked out number 3 and Angler 41 has 4. By grand deduction Pedestrian must be betwixt us!

So let's rush to our angle rods and await the shout.

PEDES: How goes it Master? As we used to say in Yorkshire, have you got amongst them?

PISC: I affirm my presence midst the shoals dear friend but alas the striking arm is much too ponderous, old bones and purblind orbits conspiring to snatch the line too late.

It's the fish that make sport of me! They mock my empty hook. The innards of the maggots are sucked clean and only flaccid skin remains ... but I may have been dozing.

I strike and the float flies through the air behind me. Why just now I tugged and the whole contraption came sailing forth, my point becoming lodged in the pyramidal mound of some snowy confection that a child was fondly licking. The poor sobbing infant almost impaled its tongue before I made a rescue and consoled the terrified mater.

But I've made one small catch, a lonely gudgeon giving me cause to wet this cavernous net and hope for more. He'll get a companion if I can curb my excitement and learn from your experience at your shadow bridge.

How goes Ephemator? Does his net bulge?

PEDES: With a cheeky grin on his face, he repels my probing but I've heard the splashing and I think he does well. But he has me and 41 to vanquish.

I must say that it's wonderfully exciting to be fishing with you today. It's a dream come true and I can't wait to tell my grandchildren.

I do hope you're enjoying yourself as well?

PISC: I'm having a whale of a time Pedestrian and if I can set the point sooner I hope to catch one.

PEDES: Your smile fills me with effervescent joy Master. I'll deposit this moment in my minds vault. Whenever the clouds roll in, it will restore me to sunshine.

Here, take this. I've brought you a flask of tea. It'll quench your thirst. I'll go back to my own peg now and hopefully catch some fish.

See you later.

ANGLER 41: I see you're smoking a pipe Mr Cotton. Here, try one of these. Take a fag.

EPHEM: A fag? Don't you think it's rather small to perform a cudgelling Sir?

Oh! I see. You insert it between the lips and ignite it. How wonderful. I can dispense with my briar and still suck on tobacco smoke.

But how fares you? Is your net pulsing with fins?

ANGLER 41: I've caught about a dozen small fish. Not bad, but nothing to cheer about. And the match is nearly over.

But I've been watching you. You handle the rod as if you were born to it. And you say it's the first time you've ever used a reel? I'm impressed. Cushty. I think you'll win the match. It's a racing cert.

I've checked and I don't think Mr Walton or Pedestrian have caught much.

I'm sure the hundred quid's yours. I might win fifty. I've caught the usual bream, perch, roach and gudgeon and I've a small eel and a lamprey as well.

And there's the shout.

That's that.

But what's this?

That must be Mr Walton calling. What's the crack?

Come on; let's run along the bank and have a shuftie.

EPHEM: Master, your rod describes the tautest longbow. You surely grapple with the biggest monster in London.

But what a sore pity Sir. The shout has echoed and the match is concluded. Land the beast forthwith – he's a pike I see! – and we'll have him complexioned by the finest taxidermist in London. Know, however, that he cannot be allowed to grace the weighing pan.

PEDES: Play him Master! Though your arms are breaking apply the side strain. He's heading for those lily pads. Hold him!

He must be a beast of ten or twelve pounds in weight.

PISC: Yes, he's a pike. Sweet Jesus he grabbed at a roach as I was reeling him in.

PEDES: Hold on Sir! We'll have him banked and stuffed yet. And you too Ephemator! Forgive me.

I'll pardon your enthusiasm but I have to tell you that you're wrong to assume that this fish cannot spin the needle for the Lee Valley Country Park Rules clearly state that any fish hooked before the closing shout's called may be landed and weighed.

EPHEM: What contrariness is this?

PEDES: And here he comes. A fine specimen of *Esox lucius.* I'll stretch out the net. What a beauty! Look at his dotted flanks of shimmering green. And there's a gape to swallow you whole.

A whale indeed!

Watch his teeth Piscator and I'll unhook him.

Fetch the scales 41 and we'll dish him first. If he plunges the dial, all the other weighing could be redundant.

There we are … 10 pounds 7 ounces … no, 10 pounds 8 ounces … and add the three gudgeon and the one small roach … 10 pounds 11 ounces in total.

I'll mark your card. Piscator, 10 pounds 11 ounces to beat. Well done!

Now, knock him on the head and we'll despatch him for mounting.

PISC: What a fish! I present him to you Pedestrian as a gift. Have him lurk in ambuscade about your parlour in the finest crystalled box, his gaze recalling yet another moment in this remarkable day.

PEDES: I'm next … but look at that. It's hardly worth the bother. I'll tip them back and they can swim away.

EPHEM: Here we are gentlemen, my draught of fishes. See how they splash, flip and writhe.

What's your opinion Master? Is it not a fine haul for a man more accustomed to the fly?

But will I overhaul your mammoth catch? I'll slide them in and we'll see.

PEDES: Nowhere near old friend. Look! The needle sticks on 7 dead. Hard luck. But you've got five species and may be in the money yet.

Come on. One to weigh. Then we'll present the prizes.

ANGLER 41: You gentlemen have brought me good luck. I've caught a lot more fish than I did yesterday.

Up they come. I reckon it 'ill be neck and neck with you Mr Cotton.

PEDES: It's flickering a bit … 7 … 7 … 3 …

EPHEM: Please Pedestrian. Would you remove that lump of mud from the perch's gill?

And retrieve the eel. He's escaping!

PEDES: Well yes … 7 … 7 pounds 2 ounces … 7 pounds 2 ounces it is. And yes; six different fish; you have the most species 41.

Pop them back and I'll do the honours.

PISC: I've done it Ephemator! The old man triumphs yet again. Oh, I'm so enjoying myself.

EPHEM: It's good to see you so effusive Master and I do grumblingly rejoice in your victory.

Viva victor!

That yonder pike has pipped us both on the line 41 but methinks Peter himself must have snapped his jaws.

So watch out Master.

We'll cross rods again in three days time on my own Pike Pool and I'll trounce you with the fly.

PEDES: Again as in the days of old, I'll don my flat cap for the announcement and presentation.

Sound the fanfare!

In first place with a weight of 10 pounds 11 ounces is Piscator! Second is 41 with 7 pounds 2 ounces. Third is Ephemator with 7 pounds and fourth with an empty net … is me.

And now, it gives me great pleasure to present the prizes.

Step up Piscator – da! da! dat! da! da! – and receive £100 for the heaviest catch and £50 for the largest fish.

Next, you 41. Congratulations. Here's £50 for catching the most species.

As for poor Ephemator.

Well, not to leave you out, here's a prize for you. We call it a booby.

Come forward and don't be shy old friend.

I honour you with not so much a fanfare as a bovine emission.

Listen while I blow.

Blusph! Plurg! Zhurk!

Please accept this flatulence whistle with compliments of the organising committee.

Look!

Even the pike's laughing!

THIRD DAY

CHAPTER TWO

Where to?

Tuesday. The Feast of St Athanasius of Athos. Early afternoon.
Holyfield Marsh, Cheshunt.

EPHEM: It's so good to see the Master's chest heaving in mirth. In coping with my perceived demeaning in the past, I'd have worn the scowling face of a Mr Punch pummelled with his own club.

But not any more. I can now guffaw with you all.

I've realised that it's the mark of a man to bear the butt of gentle humour as a deep-throated cavern, so that the precious strains of laughter can be echoed and magnified.

In my past life, I was too much of a prig and dandy to appreciate the rudeness of your penny plaything but not now. Enlightenment has pinpricked my pride like a balloon and I can chortle with the rest.

Look at the Master. He strides out and is walking on air. Let's catch him.

PEDES: Wait for us!

It seems that the encounter with your whale has not fatigued you too much?

Sorry for the delay but I've been making arrangements with 41. He'll take your fish to the taxidermist's.

But continue prancing. It's around 8 miles to Ware.

PISC: Where?

PEDES: Ware.

PISC: Where?

PEDES: Ware.

Enough!

We need to curtail this thrust and parry before my publisher runs out of pages and the spittle dries in my throat.

Where going to Ware.

It's famous for its bed you know. Constructed in oak around 1590 when you were but a child, it's ten feet wide and can accommodate twelve sleepers. Unfortunately, it's been relocated from a local tavern to a museum in London so we three will have to make do with single rooms again.

PISC: Shame.

PEDES: But I suppose it's just as well with Ephemator and his whistle on the prowl.

Just listen to him! There he blows!

And hear the ducks. They think it's a mating call!

PISC: Our jollity is the finest tonic wine.

I complain not but I think three centuries of absolute peace and serenity have sometimes made me a dull fellow. I'd forgotten just how it feels to snort and tremble in uproarious pain and to sense the dampness in my under garments.

Laughter fuels contentment and well-being and is a prescription for the world.

I laughed my hose off yesterday and I've laughed again today but I better compose my face lest I have a hernia.

PEDES: I'm invigorated by your buoyant words and gaiety Master.

Tell me, what will you do with your prize money?

PISC: I'll tell you in an instant.

Hurry on Ephemator!

Open your hand and accept this £50 from me and know that your merriment is worth a hundred times more.

And here's £50 for you as well Pedestrian!

Good fortune should be shared with good friends.

Besides – I can't take it with me!

PEDES: Thank you Master, I appreciate the gift but with your permission, I'll donate the money to a worthy cause. I'm sure in the days ahead we'll find a suitable recipient.

EPHEM: A splendid notion Pedestrian! I pledge my £50 to boot.

PISC: 'Tis decided then and my £50 also.

But the winning was the thing and thank you again Pedestrian for organising our contest. It was very enjoyable.

That was my first experience of match fishing but you must have participated in many more?

As we amble along, please acquaint us with more tales of your Yorkshire match fishing outings.

You've already mentioned the evocatively named Kirk Hammerton. It sounds a pastoral place?

PEDES: Kirk Hammerton, Cowthorpe, Nun Monkton, Ulleskelf, Spennithorne, Summerbridge, Helperby, Buttercrambe, Yedingham and many others. When I allow my tongue to linger on the words I recite poetry.

At the time I first went match fishing, I was a teenager living with my mother and father in a back-to-back house in the heart of Leeds, a vast northern city famous for its clothing manufacture and heavy engineering. My home was surrounded on all sides by noisy factories with their coppices of belching chimneys and by serried rows of similar houses with cobbled streets between. At the ends of the rows were privy blocks that were frozen up in winter. In summer they reeked of excrement and disinfectant and were invaded by clouds of midges. As children, we played games in the streets, teasing out tar that oozed between the cobbles on hot days, scribbling ribald verses on the walls of neighbouring houses with chalks stolen from headmaster's desk and firing our bows and arrows at the lines of washing that hung like prayer flags, imploringly flapping for a better age.

When older, we wandered beyond our corners to explore the railway marshalling yards and the derelict school that had been damaged by bombs in the last world war against the Germans.

Apart from rank stands of rosebay willow herb that seemed to flourish amongst the fly-tipped spoil and crumbling masonry, nothing seemed to grow in our far-flung outpost of Arcadia but fishing changed all my perceptions.

One minute I existed in a monochrome world regulated by the sounds of klaxons, grinding wheels and rattling looms and was choking on smoke smelling of coal and hot metal. Then, moments later I was sniffing wild red roses and staring disbelieving at a translucent river that had a remarkable absence of dead dogs and oil scum.

It was that same Charlie I spoke of earlier who introduced me to match fishing. He somehow managed to retain his job with the clothing company and he joined their fishing club, introducing me as a member when I was just twelve or thirteen. The club organised a dozen or so matches every year at various venues, renting a bus for around thirty anglers each trip. At the time, working men on low incomes found it difficult to buy cars, so the opportunities of visiting faraway country places to fish beyond the reach of the noise and pollution of the city were roundly seized. There was a waiting list to join the C&M Sumrie Angling Club.

Most of the club members worked six days a week so all the matches were on Sunday. My preparations would begin the day before when I'd walk into town to a tackle shop. There I'd by my maggots and sundries such as line, hooks, floats and lead weights. The maggots were sold by the pint glass and came in three varieties – natural white and dyed red and yellow. They were brought in from specialist suppliers who used condemned abattoir animal livers for the breeding. Somehow, they managed to remove the overpowering stench of rancid flesh and ammonia.

The maggots were so inoffensive that some of my angling chums, by way of enlivenment, put the grubs under their tongues on a winter's morning.

PISC: 'Tis a pity they weren't around when I first trod the banks. I would have been spared the grief and torment of two complaining wives, both spouses vehemently railing at my maggot breeding with corpses of dead sheep. If you enquired obligingly, there was sometimes a rotting carcase to be had from the shambles along Fleet Street.

PEDES: As a somewhat shy and retiring boy, I sometimes missed my turns in the queues that formed in the shop on those busy afternoons, always deferring to those well-known fellows who were renown for their skill with rod and line, their scale-stained jackets and cow-clap caps adorned with multiple badges marking them out as experts.

On the nights before our outings, dreams of bobbing floats gave me little rest and I always awoke at sunrise, joining my wonderful parents for breakfast as we prepared to go to early mass. After our meal we'd walk to St Patrick's Church, mother tenderly holding my rods and father carrying an old wicker creel that has seen long and cherished service. Following communion and the final *pax vobiscum,* I'd walk to the rendezvous point to join my good friend Mick on the street corner, both parents waiting with me until the bus arrived, me wriggling to escape a farewell kiss as the doors opened and we stepped inside to cheers and ribald salutations.

Invariably, and you'll warm to this Ephemator, there was always what we called a card school underway, ten shilling and one pound notes flying around as fast as the kings and queens.

We'd quickly leave the suburbs and drive on between green fields into the countryside, the club secretary, who usually occupied an honoured reserved seat behind the drivers cab, getting to his feet and wobbling down the aisle to collect the sweepstakes from each angler.

The atmosphere in the bus was usually impregnated with farmyard odours and sometimes discernible rising steam, clothing and boots that had not seen laundry baskets for a month of those Sundays, sweating and heaving almost as much as the million or so maggots that by this time on the Sabbath were beginning to acquire their trade mark pongs.

The hardly breathable air was further tinged blue by a certain ripe coarseness of language and banter between the anglers, some men bragging about the previous night's sexual conquests and others about their prowess in sinking multiple gallons of ale.

I'd previously seen some of these voluble types in local shops and precincts. There, in usual henpecked mode, they'd follow in the penumbras of their all-dominating wives with heads bent in thralled silence and in total subjugation to admonishing eyes and fingers. But then for a few glorious hours in the week they blossomed like day lilies, dams full of quips and obscenities that had been held back since the previous Sunday bursting forth to be lapped up by the men like thirsty dogs.

Those men were rough types who'd use every type of ruse and obfuscation to keep their angling secrets, but do you know Master, I'd be proud to introduce you to them now. If you ever found yourself in trouble they'd be first to offer you their help or hard earned cash. Those men were the salt of the earth.

By and by, we left the roar of the main highways and began weaving through rustic lanes, always fetching up, unerringly, at a country inn. Like your rosy-cheeked and attentive milk maids of old, the ladies of those quiet vales had been afoot since dawn and they greeted us as we filed through the doors of the *Crown Inn* or the *Ye Olde Oak* to gobble up their bacon butties and to drink copious amounts of tea. Sometimes, two or even three buses would descend on those sleepy villages simultaneously, the amply bosomed victuallers setting up their stalls and urns outside on trestle tables, large queues shuffling forward in ripening tweeds and rubber boots.

The atmosphere in the lines was always lively and good-natured but as the match time approached, each man would become more reflective and self absorbed, wandering off abstractedly to resume his seat for the final drive to the bank. Once there, the draw for pegs would commence, the honourable secretary spinning round his cap in the manner I imitated this morning and then reciting the rules before beginning the serious business of the draw.

Some men who had an intimate knowledge of the river and knew which peg numbers were most likely to yield large hauls of fish, put in their thumbs and, like beaming Little Jack Horners, pulled out plum lies. The scowls of others betrayed the likelihood of dry nets.

The match hours had the feel of a convocation of monks, cowled in prayer. In total concentration, few anglers spoke or left their pegs to converse with their neighbours, the onset of rain adding an extra anonymity as the men retreated under hoods and umbrellas.

I have to admit that, at times like that, young Mick and I found match fishing quite boring especially if you'd drawn a peg with few fish. On some outings, especially when the wind blew and the heavens opened, it was akin to being struck dumb and bed ridden to writhe and flounder in sodden blankets.

For you must understand that Mick and I had mischief in our blood, a humorous quip or a practical joke usually parting clouds on even the foulest days. But what we did with our young friends on more casual fishing trips was strictly proscribed on match days.

So we just sat there.

We grimaced and bore it. And even when we stared at our floats for hours with not a tremble and the damp crept up our stockings and started invading our under pants to consort with converse trickles from the north, we still remained silent and stoical.

We defied ennui and keep fishing.

Oh Master you would have been so proud of us!

Never once did we resort to lobbing stones in our fellow anglers swims on the pretence of a rise.

Never once did we hurl ripely dripping elderberries down open neck shirts.

Never once did we, at times when our neighbours were relieving themselves, take up their floats to affix jelly babies to their hooks.

And not on a single occasion did we throw handfuls of maggots into fellow competitors fishing baskets to wriggle and to secrete themselves and to metamorphose in dark corners, on the fortnightly anniversaries of the throwing to take wing and terrorise households in dense swarms.

No and emphatically no. Angelic Mick and I did none of those things on the certainty of finding ourselves stripped naked, whipped with nettle stalks and chopped into delicious fishy cubes that would neatly fit into an Oxo tin.

But we were not always bored. Why, I once won a match with a prize gudgeon!

You should have witnessed the contorted faces of men who had spent a week in busy preparation and had lavished a fortune on bait and equipment. See them glower when they examined my two shillings rod and rusty reel!

Yes, I sometimes liked the match fishing.

And, after the weigh in, all the contestants would shuffle back to the inn for a celebratory or consolatory glass of ale, Mick and I satisfying our thirsts with ginger beer.

Eventually, the bus would head back to the city, the effluvial vapours, smelling of sweat, fish-mucus and beer, percolating from its slipstream.

A few of the old timers – they'd been let out for the day by hawk-eyed wives – would be delivered home like overdue parcels. As the hour was usually exceptionally late and the old gentlemen rather inebriated, Mick and I were delegated escort duties. Following instructions, we were to take them to their doors where we'd prop them up and rap the knockers before proceeding to rush back to the safety of the bus.

Finally, we'd both limp home to anxious parents, the following day at school bragging about our adventures to our friends who'd had ordinary Sundays playing games.

PISC: And what of my assertion that God never made a more innocent recreation than angling? Methinks your match fishing was anchor to a sail that ever sought the wind. You were a flighty kingfisher, not a heron Pedestrian but that be no counter to misdemeanour. You and little Mick risketh becoming chub meat even amongst your friends!

PEDES: No Master. Like Chick Minor, we were good little boys.

PISC: You were a rascal Sir! Go on. Admit it!

I see it in a smile that endures a half-century. It still illuminates your face on the memory.

PEDES: I blush on your reproach but know Master that I divulged my misdemeanours in the dark confessional and was forgiven.

And I've hardly tossed a pebble since childhood and, surely, my skill at flinging elderberries has not been tested in decades. Why, this very morning I resisted the temptation and left your collar clean!

PISC: It's as well Pedestrian or take note that I myself would have filled that Oxo tin.

Now let's march on to Ware.

PEDES: Where?

THIRD DAY

CHAPTER THREE

Custard tarts and a faceless God

Tuesday. The Feast of St Athanasius of Athos. Early afternoon.
Broxbourne Mill, Broxbourne.

PEDES: We're making excellent time gentlemen so let's tarry for a while beside this old mill. It was here at the time of Domesday. Unfortunately, the building succumbed to a fire in 1949 only some charred timbers and the mill wheel remaining.

EPHEM: But this plaque applauds a resurrection in 2001, the mill wheel turning still.

PISC: Why, what memory! Although I stumble in the recall of last evening's food-stuffs, I remember this halcyon spot with dazzling clarity for I once caught a fat perch hereabouts on a dead mouse that had been making free with my flour sacks.

And what chalk and cheese. Compared to those shadowed banks back there, this backwater is infused with the rhythms of my old meads and the lilting echoes of my favourite milkmaids, those young boys under the willows fishing contentedly while their parents drink tea at yonder shack.

Can we partake of some refreshment Pedestrian? I've given you all my money!

Could we please impose on the munificence of your purse once more?

PEDES: Of course. We'll sit at the tables and talk for a while, letting the world drift by.

EPHEM: I know you're invigorated and contented Master? But is our journey delivering the promises we made?

PISC: It is my friend and Pedestrian – just look at him at that counter – is such an affable and animated soul that every moment seems filled with new experiences and opportunities to fulfil our compact. The only problem is, that the hours rush by and for these seven days we're governed by that timepiece on your wrist. You must return it to Pedestrian on our parting. We've no need for such devices up there.

Observe our host's humour even in the procurement of our tea.

Why, thank you Pedestrian … and what's this?

PEDES: It's a treat, I've not tasted since I was a young schoolboy, the sight of these custard tarts making me feel as though I ought to pay a belated visit to my old confessional, remembering to keep the Oxo tin out of sight.

I've already obtained your absolution for the tricks Mick and I played on our fishing match chums, so I suppose I need to make a clean breast of it and tell you the tale of the custard tarts.

PISC: It might go someway into easing your entry into eternity but the passageway becomes narrower with each revelation does it not Ephemator?

EPHEM: Just so Master. Spare not the details while we gobble up our own tarts Pedestrian.

PEDES: Imagine the scene. Dinnertime in the school dining hall. From above, let your attention fix on a table, opposing rows of four hungry boys on benches confronting each other, sixteen swivelling, eager eyes focusing on a newly delivered eight-portioned platter of custard tart. The most innocent looking boy in the whole assembly shuffles to a central, carefully chosen strategic position just inches away from the tart. He checks to make sure that the supervising teachers are out of earshot and barks a call for the proceedings to begin, the single utterance 'Scramble!' unleashing a frenzy of spoon delving, each boy shovelling as much of the mother load into his bowl as he can, the clash of cutlery, the flying pastry, the bespattering gobbets of custard, the woeful cries of the boys on the table ends whose arms are not long enough to ensure even a mouthful and the practiced gobblings of the architects of this piranha feast conspiring to create a quick-fire metal-clashing, profanity ripe orgy, reducing the platter to a crumbed emptiness in seconds.

PISC: Shall we relocate to the next table Ephemator? It may be wise.

I'm afeard that an Oxo tin might not be quite big enough Pedestrian. If you were that innocent announcer, all the sackcloth's and ashes in the kingdom might not widen the pathways.

But we'll pray for you my friend as we guard our sweetmeats in cupped hands.

In mitigation though, I could possibly explain to the Gatekeeper why you acted so and, in the sacrifice of this sharing, suggest that you're a reformed fellow.

Yes, these tarts are pure ambrosia.

PEDES: I was speedily reformed as soon as the supervising teachers caught sight of our antics, a personal lug- cuffing, a presentation before the headmaster and six strokes of *Doctor Cure 'Em Quick* mending my ways quicker than any confessional box admonitions from Father Keogh.

I'm a good boy I am!

So let's sup up. I want to take you the short distance to another church you may remember? St Augustine's is just up the lane.

PISC: Is it still there? On inclement days when the rain lashed the river, I would oft times take shelter in its nave eating my bread and cheese by the effigies of Sir Henry Cock and his wife.

I had an affinity with that family. The figures of the infants at the base of the monument were macabre symbols of the widespread infant mortality that was such a scourge of our times.

Like those grieving parents, I lost many children.

PEDES: Come Master be cheerful. Though the church was rebuilt and enlarged before 1460, its fabric and the ancient Cock tomb are both in good repair and are lovingly cared for by the modern parishioners.

Just a few yards more. The church sits prettily overlooking an expansive village green.

Shall we venture inside, perhaps praying for a few moments?

EPHEM: It's heart warming to observe such cherishment of these old stones and monuments. Our Christian religion truly survives.

But as we yesterday passed through London town, we both noted the many notice boards proclaiming the tabernacles of other religious groups – Roman Catholics, Methodists, Quakers, Baptists, Presbyterian and Jews – you explaining Pedestrian that even within a few miles of St Paul's there are now places of hallowed worship for Muslims, Hindus and Buddhists

What are we to make of this Master?

PISC: Just a few minutes ago, you asked me about the fulfilling of our compact.

The utterance of the words I'm about to say is a prime condition of that compact, only the most appropriate time and place hitherto delaying the speaking.

What site could be more fitting than at the rails of Henry Cock's tomb?

I have to tell you and your readers this dear Pedestrian.

Although I was an Anglican ready to lay down my life on the perceived sole route to God, centuries of reflection and correction impel me now to impart a wisdom that must henceforth cause all men to assemble on a single road.

Please light three candles Ephemator to illuminate this special moment and please Pedestrian, hear my humble words with your own humility and understanding.

All the aforementioned religions, my own included, still wander on the fractured byways of the spiritual path. Every seeker must, from this moment forth, come together, realising that the only one true religion is a personal relationship with God forged inside the soul. Henceforth, every seeker of the light must gently extricate himself free of all distracting texts, scriptures, incantations, icons and rituals. And all good men should know that although the countenance of God is, to humankind, Janus-like with a thousand faces, ultimately our one true Master is the faceless vanishing point of creation and all eternity.

But I am much encouraged.

Two days past, we visited the church of St James in Piccadilly. There, I pocketed a card that says this:

St James's is part of the Anglican communion within the world wide Christian church. We understand ourselves to be called to create a space where people of any faith or none can question and discover the sacred in life through openness, struggle and laughter and prayer.

Shall we kneel gentlemen and pray that this may be so?

THIRD DAY

CHAPTER FOUR

The Fish and Eels

Tuesday. The Feast of St Athanasius of Athos. Mid- afternoon.
Near Dobb's Weir Bridge, Nazeing Mead.

PISC: A thought is bubbling to my brow as we march along past this lock. Apart from the pleasant chuggings of those colourful narrow boats and the occasional swish of passing cyclists, all is silent here.

You've told us that nearly eight million people reside in this great capital Pedestrian.

So, where might they be?

PEDES: I've been thinking the same.

Do you know something? I've recently walked the 268 miles of the Pennine Way, a wild and lonely route along the spine of England from Edale in your old county of Derbyshire Ephemator, going north to the village of Kirk Yetholm in Scotland.

I saw few fellow hikers on my journey, but even less here.

Where is everybody?

EPHEM: They're all about their various businesses, rushing hither and thither and not knowing what to do when they get there.

Is humankind impelled to coalescence?

PISC: An instinct to morbid congress draws our populations into the cities where, denied his home turf, a man must erect a fence and plant a lonesome pine.

PEDES: In our little city house we never had even a window box.

My father always abhorred what he termed as 'pushing and shoving' and he walked everywhere, always escaping the crowds.

I must have inherited some of his instincts, for as soon as I could read, I homed in on the writings of the men whose kind words have put me here and I began seeking out the quiet places.

It was that great environmentalist John Muir – truly your natural successor Master – who wrote: 'Break clear away once in awhile and climb a mountain or spend a week in the woods.'

He suggested that the natural world is a conductor of divinity, knowing that one day's exposure to mountain peaks is worth a cartload of books.

I spent nearly three weeks last June with my dear friend Bernard in traversing my own mountains.

'Nature's peace will flow into you as the sunshine flows into trees,' remarked John. 'The winds will blow their freshness into you and storms their energy, while cares will drop off like autumn leaves.'

And they did. And next year, Bernard and I, having re-read John's *A Thousand-Mile*

Walk to the Gulf might step out for three months!

EPHEM: Your spouse must be particularly understanding Pedestrian?

PEDES: She knows I keep the very best company my friend and besides, we have a telepathic empathy that defies any separation.

EPHEM: Does she know you're about to enter a pub? Some women can be contrary on such matters.

PEDES: She knows I cross the threshold of one of my favourite old inns, and applauds my enterprise knowing that my two hot and thirsty companions gape like the swinging fish above.

I do so love a traditional inn sign.

Look! The sea dog rows fast ashore with a fine catch on his planks.

Come, gentlemen, I've reserved a table on the terrace overlooking the river.

We'll eat the rower's catch!

PISC: It seems a most appropriate thing to do in an inn so named.

And what is that chalked on the menu board but one of my own favoured treats? I've not tasted crayfish since I was a young man.

But like our restaurant salmon, will it be farmed?

PEDES: No Master, it'll have been plucked from under our very noses from the Lea.

And by eating the dish, you'll be helping the environment.

PISC: How so?

PEDES: The menu dish is the American or signal crayfish. As with many things you've seen today – the Himalayan balsam, the grey squirrel and the collared dove – the species is not native to this country, but was imported. It's much bigger than our English crayfish and spreads a contagion that threatens our indigenous white claw.

By gobbling it up you'll be encouraging the capture of more of the blighters, enabling those most enterprising of Lea anglers to buy more wicker pots and in the crunching saving a threatened creature.

PISC: Well then, crayfish it is, contagion and all.

EPHEM: I should also like to contribute to the eradication.

I'll have the same waiter.

PEDES: And me too. And can we have three pints of Kentish ale to wash the crayfish down?

Now, what do you think of this splendid view gentlemen?

I personally think it's the finest spot on the whole river, those anglers choosing the banks of Arcadia.

PISC: It's very picturesque. A man could linger here for days and wallow contentedly, falling asleep at his rodside.

EPHEM: In hot weather such as this, our haven is pure perfection.

And even here – deliciously so – there's hardly a soul abroad.

I too have an inclination to steer into the backwaters preferred by your pater, thoughts of your journey north and your love for the lonely hills bringing to mind my old poem – *The Retirement*. Some of its lines allude to a cave in Dovedale where I often sought solace.

If the feeble embers of recollection can be fanned by concentration, may I recite several dustily perceived snatches for you as an entertainment while we await our meal?

Dear solitude the souls best friend … to walk to ride, sit or sleep at one's own ease and pleasing a man's self, none other to displease.

O my beloved caves! from dog-star's heat, and all anxieties my safe retreat.

Lord! Would men let me alone what an ever-happy one should I think myself to be. Might I in this desert place which most men in discourse disgrace, live but undisturb'd and free! Here, in this despis'd recess would I maugre winter's cold and the summer's worst excess try to live out sixty full years old! And, all the while, without an envious eye on any thriving under Fortune's smile, contented live and then contented die.

PEDES: A very impassioned and revealing poem Ephemator, thank you.

Your brain sifting excites my own capture – a memory of several lines written by my namesake Gervase Markham – and the sight of those contented fishermen – bringing forth these ancient words:

An angler must be full of love, both to his pleasure and to his neighbour; to his pleasure, which otherwise will be irksome and tedious; and to his neighbour, that he never give offence in any particular, nor be guilty of any destruction.

He should not be unskilful in music, that whenever either melancholy, heaviness of his thoughts or the perturbation of his own fancies, stirreth up sadness in him, he may remove the same with some godly hymn or anthem.

PISC: If I were sadness down I would sing you an anthem. I am, however, ecstatic and exalted.

In your own words, Pedestrian, Wackford Squeers!

PEDES: Wackford Squeers gentlemen!

No, indeed, we've no need of a godly hymn but rather a livelier tune.

You wont believe this … but voila! Look at what I pluck from my backpack.

Another surprise!

Thanks waiter – they look very appetising. More salt and pepper on those gentlemen?

Do you remember me telling you on Sunday that I'd bought something in the Izaak Walton Cottage that would entertain you? Well, on the cusp of the moment, this disc has been patiently biding its entry. I'll slip it in the player I've carried concealed in my pack and you'll listen to the most appropriate musical accompaniment to a feast ever written.

The composer was as inspired by your great book as I was when he set its pages to music.

What will you make of *Songs from the Compleat Angler by* Paul Brett?

PISC: ♬ The-gallant-fisher's-life-is-the-best-of-any. The-gallant-fisher's-life-is-loved-by-so-many ♫

The refrain is swirling round in my mind like yonder eddy.

PEDES: You sing beautifully Master. But who could have imagined the scene?

One minute we were alone claw-crunching and the next, why, every angler on the Lea must have laid down their rods and joined us.

But where did the man with the guitar come from?

EPHEM: He sallied forth from the direction of the kitchen, his snow-white apparel suggesting a culinary trade.

And all those foaming tankards. What was their provenance? And who paid the potman?

If I'd consumed another drop, I'd be floating to Ware.

PEDES: Where?

PISC: ♬ In-the-morning-when-we-rise-before-the-sun's-a peeping. We-wake-and-wash-our-eyes-and-leave-the-world-a sleeping ♫

I'm so, so happy Pedestrian! What a feast of a day you've laid before us. Passion, profundity and pure, button-popping pleasure in the few short hours since breakfast.

Am I not in good form?

And the sun is yet high!

Every yard of this path is intoxicating and it's not just your Kentish ale dripping off my tongue.

What's next?

PEDES: You both may have noticed that I hurried you by the *Jolly Fisherman* at Stanstead Abbotts? It's a fine alehouse and they have a rather impressive glass case barbel above the bar that's worth seeing.

But, if your excesses lead to a premature return to the pearly gates, you'd not want to meet a grim-faced St Peter brandishing a breathalyser. Would you?

If that happened, my own copybook would be well and truly blotted and stamped ENTRY REFUSED!

No, for the next hour or so – we'll turn right here over the bridge – and enjoy the Amwell Nature Reserve. After years of noise and disruption in the winning of mountains of sand and gravel, it's now a haven for wildlife, the nourishing flow of our friend Lea giving it life and creating a habitat for 210 species of birds and a home for our old friend the otter.

We'll walk the short distance to the hide down there and with legerdemain, I'll produce another marvel of the age from my pack.

What will you make of my high-powered binoculars?

THIRD DAY

CHAPTER FIVE

The greatest gift

Tuesday. The Feast of St Athanasius of Athos. Evening. The Trysting Tree Hotel, Ware.

PISC: Hello gentlemen!

I'm so happy and enamoured of seeing you both even though we've been apart but one hour. But I'm well rested.

Verily, this blessed day has been one of the best of my second life and indubitably, even one of the choicest of the first.

So, as the evening is so clement, let's remove ourselves to the terrace by the Lea to sit amongst the flowers and the late rays of sun.

PEDES: You're happy Master. I'm so very pleased.

EPHEM: I am most contented as well Pedestrian.

But here on earth, happiness can be a transient and fleeting gift that's seldom nourished until it vanishes like hot dew.

PISC: But it need not be so.

PEDES: But how? And, can I ask you again? What is happiness Master and why do men seek it in fishing?

You gaze into the water with such inquiring eyes.

PISC: Happiness is a total contentment with what is and a banishment of all desires, angling, like no other sport or pastime, infusing a glorious detachment from the artificial and ultimately meaningless cares of man. An angler may leave his troubles at the river stile, suspending pride and pettiness and all inclinations to control and dominate, immersing himself instead to be as one with the wonders of the natural world.

EPHEM: When the braying creditors were queuing at my door I did immerse myself Master – but alas nearly too deeply!

The hounds were tearing at my pockets but they were sore empty and I raged with fear and loathing, examining the frothy tide of my Dove in spate for a quick release.

But there on the brink, I remembered your haunting and oft-repeated words on happiness and your recitation on the parable of the talents and I stood back shaking with cold and fear, the wisdom and warmth of your friendship, the love of my family, the encouraging words of the many fellows who had read my poems with fond appreciation and the joy of the man who only that morning had lifted my latch to praise my tying of the Harry Long Legs, all pulling me to firmer ground.

Verily I agree with your sentiments on happiness Master.

And would you believe that this peacock became the drabbest bird whilst angling.

PEDES: But you're a handsome fellow Sir. What do you mean?

EPHEM: I was sometimes cocksure and arrogant Pedestrian. Born to riches and privilege I swaggered through life adorning myself like that fabled bird. I wore slipper shoes, silks, embroidered linens, gorgeous plumes, puffed-up pantaloons and flowing periwigs that had a dozen women all a-balding, my entire ensemble sniffing as bad as that odour on your match day bus! Why I virtually bathed in French cologne, the stink sending even the foulmart scuttling!

Before I became a true convert to the ways of angling, I'd pose and preen in front of my looking glass, peering this way and that, plumping up my feathers on my best side. I'd adore my refection as Narcissus, prancing in exultation of a self-love that bred disdain and haughtiness.

But angling presented a different mirror.

Know this, that slipper shoes are unsuited to muddy ground. Off with them!

Know this, that silks, embroidered linens, gorgeous plumes and puffed-up pantaloons, snag on bankside twigs and brambles and send a message to trout that a predator far more sparkling than a maharajah's elephant stalks the pools. Off with them!

And know this, that flowing periwigs tend to restrict the proper operation of your casting arm and, that the garment when soggy has the inclination to smother you like an amorous octopus, its dissolved perfume of jasmine and rose petals polluting the stream every bit as badly as that offending ochre mill. Off with it!

What indeed was I left with except an expanse of rather pimply skin?

Well, I'll tell you dear friends.

I was left with my true self, that altered image allowing me to become a better man with a truer appreciation of happiness although I never truly achieved it.

PISC: You were coming close when I left you in 1683 Ephemator. Do you recall the conversations we had as I faded?

Let me air them again for Pedestrian and his readers.

I feel charged to recite the age-old maxim and, dear Pedestrian, please set this down in chiselled stone. Know that all problems emanate from the mind of man.

There is nothing bad. Only mankind makes it so.

And answer me this? Are people of your generation with all your abundance and sophistication any happier than when Ephemator and I first strode the banks?

PEDES: I have to answer you a confused no Master, the same old divers conflicts, anxieties and lack of meaning and purpose still afflicting every people and country across the world.

PISC: And methinks nothing will ever change in another four hundred or even four thousand years.

Unless, unless there's a fundamental change in perception and attitude.

But forgive me dear consort.

I see by your fixed and rapt attention that you're expecting me to divulge the secrets of all the ages not withstanding the divine embargo that curtails my tongue. I cannot do this.

A myriad gurus and enlightened men have polished the same pearls since the dawn of time and no words of mine can add one jot to their learning. But know this.

Happiness is in appreciating and relishing existence hour by precious hour. It lies in taking nourishment from those hours and in nurturing the goodness so that it can be magnified and diffused like sunbeams.

Focus on your existence Pedestrian and practice to be positive and good, fashioning your appreciation every day as do the keenest apprentices in wood and stone.

And remember that our human existence is but as a single day and that you're allotted one orbit around the sun that is our all-nourishing Saviour.

Now, let us be off to our meal.

'Tis a pity you've despatched my pike.

We could have dined on him.

FOURTH DAY

CHAPTER ONE

Angling Neanderthal style

Wednesday. The Feast of St Goar. Dawn. The Trysting Tree Hotel, Ware.

PISC: Quiet Pedestrian. Close the door softly. I don't want to wake our friend from his slumbers. We spoke long and eloquently last evening after our dining and he's still sleepy.

Come. We'll creep downstairs lest we disturb the other guests.

But tell me pray. What is this angling experiment you speak of?

You avow that it was last performed before the dawn of time!

PEDES: It's just a frivolous amusement Master that appeals to my boyish ways. Indulge me please and let's amble a short distance to the river.

If my spouse has followed my instructions and found the right holly bush on the left bank, the tackle for our fun should be well concealed.

PISC: As ever, you intrigue and delight me Sir and the expectation is worth missed sleep.

Away!

Keep up Pedestrian!

PEDES: Here we are. Laid under the bush as promised, the wherewithal to lure a fish employing only plant material – including the line and hook and our disguises.

It's a whimsical endeavour but it appeals to my back-woods spirit and is symbolic of my attitudes to conservation and our need to harmonise with nature.

I've long wanted to try the experiment but I've waited for this moment.

Humour me Master.

Who could be a better companion for the trial?

And note this. I'll not even plunder horsetails.

PISC: But how will it work? Even my primitive ensemble made use of horsehair and iron hooks.

PEDES: I've done it Master by grappling with hazel sticks, bramble stems and wild rose thorns to make devices that ancient man might have used to catch his supper.

Why, I've even used a Stone Age axe of my own making to do the chopping, for authenticity in my undertaking is everything in this, I admit it, rather eccentric enterprise.

I started by cutting myself a length of hazel rod, putting aside my wood plane and taking off its bark with dry sand. Next, I took several long bramble stems and laid them out on the road, rolling them under the soles of my clogged feet back and forth to remove the thorns. Rendered harmless, the stem fibres were teased apart and each strand was twisted and knotted and coated in pine resin. The briar thorn was whittled to a hook shape with a knife made from a sliver of obsidian I once collected from the slopes of a volcano on the island of Tenerife – I never throw anything away! – and finally, a barb was cut. And then the whole thing was put together – as you now see.

PISC: I'm truly nonplussed Pedestrian.

But what pray do you intend to do with these orbs of willow?

PEDES: Indulge me Master and don't join the mallards in mockery. The leaves are intended to clothe our heads and shoulders. Such is my affection for the Green Man that we'll transmute ourselves into mythical twin brothers to aid our deceit.

Please, use this flattened stick to dig up a worm to complete our tackle, to be then unfurled and dangled from the stout bough of yonder willow.

PISC: I'm gratified that my long absence from this world makes any recognition by passers-by unlikely, although that cow examines us with a puzzled gaze.

We look rather clownish in our headdresses. Do we not?

PEDES: It's better than some of those floppy, wide brimmed hats I've seen you wearing in the old engravings. At least it blends in with the vegetation.

Can we hold the rod together Master?

What a thrill this is for me! I'm trembling.

Let the worm drop gently into that slack water behind the boulder.

There!

PISC: Quiet Pedestrian. Stop breathing so fast. You alarm the beast. He hath the interest on him.

Hold it … hold it… now strike!

You have him! Pull him out!

Wow, he's a respectable fish, one that your Neanderthal Man would have been proud of.

Now, I wonder how that creature made fire using just three sticks?

PEDES: Surely we'll spare our catch's demise Master, fearful that I'll be exhausted in the rubbing?

Do let's put him back for I've had some fun and proved my point and you are the supreme witness.

I think you'll agree that our experiment clearly demonstrates that our forefather apes were not all clubs and fornication? And I'm so gratified that at a time of national economic crisis, it sends out a clear message that our species can exist, if not on a shoestring, then certainly on a length of bramble.

So let's return to Ephemator and our breakfast.

PISC: Before we go, allow me borrow the device that captures your image.

Hold the fish up. And the rod.

Do I press here?

My! The view from the tiny window makes my chest heave in spasms!

You do look ridiculous Pedestrian.

But methinks you must discard your bonnet before we depart lest we be partaking of greens with our kippers.

I'm as hungry as a hawk.

FOURTH DAY

CHAPTER TWO

A river runs through it

Wednesday. The Feast of St Goar. Early morning. The Trysting Tree Hotel, Ware.

EPHEM: Good morning gentlemen. You both radiate the sun and the complexions of satisfied anglers. I do hope you fared well?

PEDES: Our excursion is admirably concluded Sir. I accomplished my task of catching a fish using only materials garnered from natural sources and the Master and a photograph will prove the point.

PISC: 'Tis so Ephemator. And what a point! Even the captor's hook was fashioned from a rose thorn.

I'm convinced that if a second flood renders mankind naked and destroys every machine on the globe, our own Pedestrian will alone survive.

What a resourceful fellow!

I'm tingling with the enjoyment of things he's shown us and with the import of our debates.

Harken to this! The pace of our glorious adventure has not slackened since the last Sabbath and I'm breathless and hungry and eager for the day ahead.

But first, what's for breakfast? My palate angles to thoughts of a kipper.

PEDES: The kippers here are sourced from the finest smokehouse in Scotland Master. I'll order three of Loch Fyne's best to set us up as kings for our journey.

The very thought reminds me of a line from Shakespeare's – I mean Bacon's – *Hamlet.*

A man may fish with a work that hath eat of a King, and eat of a fish that fed on a worm.

This promises to be a day of bright contrasts.

EPHEM: You've teased us since we were sepulchre sprung Pedestrian although I admit that the pudding has always been sweeter for the blindfold of anticipation.

But tell us. What are these contrasts and what next? I know we're to journey north to my homeland? But by what means?

PEDES: I'll obfuscate no longer and lay the splendid scene before you.

After we've dined, a special vehicle will collect us at this hotel and we'll be driven to Derbyshire. Our way will be via two of the nation's busiest motorways, the London Orbital – you've already made your acquaintances with the M25 – and the M1. You'll see a myriad vehicles along these routes all impelled by drivers who want to get to their destinations before they've set off! Every inch of these roads is occupied by screaming cars, vans and lorries all seemingly intent on achieving the maximum speed. And what do the drivers of these machines do when they've arrived nerve jangled and spitting brimstone and fury? Why, they kick off their shoes and utilise the few minutes they've saved by becoming bored and listless, craving something to do!

But I vent my spleen so please pardon my outrage gentlemen.

In your time, the hazardous journey north on rutted tracks would have taken several days. Nowadays, we'll have you there in but a few hours, although the flashing scenery from your vehicle's windows is poor comparison with the ancient picturesque captured by the artists of old. But it's no matter for I've plans to divert your ears and take your eyes from the road so that you'll experience nothing of the noise or the rush and rumble.

I mentioned that we'd travel in a special vehicle. In fact our carriage is a small bus fitted with a back seats viewing screen. On our journey you'll be entertained with a modern film gentlemen. And the film couldn't be more appropriate for our venture. It's called *A River Runs Through It.*

PIC: Its subject is surely near to our hearts Pedestrian. Is it an angler's film?

PEDES: It's a film that reverberates with the passions that empower my search for your *Compleat Angler*. The film is based on a semi-autobiographical novella by American angling author Norman Maclean and is set in the town of Missoula Montana in the 1920's. Maclean was a Presbyterian minister who believed that fishing was an art form, the drive to perfection in casting a fly – yes he was a strict fly fisherman Ephemator – raising his consciousness to a level whereby he could clearly understand God and all His Creation.

The concept will sound familiar Piscator.

I'll not tell you much more about the film – I don't want to spoil your enjoyment – except to say that in the book, the minister is rather disparaging of you Master.

PISC: Is he really? What does he write?

PEDES: He offers this and I quote: 'Izaak Walton is not a respectable writer. He was an Episcopalian and a bait fisherman.'

Don't laugh too loud Ephemator!

And there's another more crude comment expressed by the character Norman – the reverend's elder son. After reading the *Compleat Angler* he fulminates to his brother Paul as follows and pardon my French Master: 'The bastard doesn't even know how to spell complete. Besides, he has songs to sing to dairymaids. Whoever saw a dairymaid on the Big Blackfoot River?' Later on he continues: 'I would like to get him for a day's fishing on the Big Blackfoot with a bet on the side.'

He might have changed his mind if he'd seen your pike!

Fresh from your triumph on the River Lea, I could perhaps ask St Peter to arrange a match Master?

Shall I order the maggots?

PEDES: Please leave the luggage. Our chauffeur will see to those.

In you get gentlemen and do wear these headphones so you can enjoy the film without interruption or distraction.

Very well, if you're both sitting comfortably, I'll start the film.

To the North Country driver!

NORMAN MACLEAN: *In our family there was no clear line between religion and fishing…*

FOURTH DAY

CHAPTER THREE

The nib spills its ink

Wednesday. The Feast of St Goar. Midday. Brailsford.

PEDES: Our destination gentlemen. This is where we alight. Our chauffer will take our luggage on to our overnight lodgings but we'll walk from Brailsford.

The route from here to Ashbourne described in Part II of your book Ephemator is now the preserve of leviathan vehicles and is not fit for pedestrian souls like us. We'd be flattened or swept aside in the insane rush to reach tomorrow today.

But all is not yet devouring wheels. I know a quiet route on footpaths to the very doors of the town.

And we have the finest day for it. How the sun shines.

EPHEM: Ashbourne. How fares my hometown? I hope it's not too disfigured by the march of progress and modernity?

PEDES: Apart from the intrusion of the boneshakers, it survives tolerably well. It's much expanded and modernised of course, but green and welcoming. And from the top of Old Hill, the ancient spire of St Oswald's Church still beckons.

Are you well Master? You look a little dazed. I suspect your limbs are stiff after our long journey? I hope you didn't find it too tedious?

PISC: No, no, I'm creaking a little and somewhat abstracted but I anticipate our walk with a rosy welcome.

No, it's the final words of your film that detain my thoughts.

'When I'm alone, eventually all things merge into one and a river runs through it. I am haunted by waters.'

Do you know, I was never distracted once on our journey here? I was so beguiled. It was a beautiful film.

Norman Maclean knew that angling is truly a window to God, a portal, and a reminder that when we loose ourselves in the stream of life, we find ourselves in the eternal.

The scene of the father and his two sons fly-fishing on the Big Blackfoot River was a metaphor for the beloved Trinity.

I was totally absorbed by the film dear Pedestrian. Once again you've filled these fleeting hours with so much joy.

You're sensitive and perceptive and so keen to fill our every moment with wonder that, when I report back, I'll tender a glowing report!

PEDES: I've had some divine promptings! But don't lay it on too thick! I'm not ready for promotion just yet!

But let's talk some more about the film as we stroll down the lane to Brailsford Green.

Did you enjoy it Ephemator?

EPHEM: I did indeed Pedestrian. I thought it was captivating. The views of the Big Blackfoot River were so lovely. The master nudged my elbow during the scene he mentioned and finally conceded that fly-fishing is the acme of our sport.

What an admission!

But I found the film unnervingly telling at least a part of my own story. I saw my life of Janus unfolding in both brothers – one a poet and the other a gambler. Norman was yoked to his father's love of literature but Paul broke free and became an artist and for those few brief hours on the Big Blackfoot River, he was as seamless as his perfect cast and, yes, he was suspended above the earth free from all its laws and troubles. Through that four-count rhythm, he indeed had a glimpse of eternal life thinking the world would flow through his veins forever. In the end though, liquor and the evils of gambling cut him down.

In one memorable scene, when Paul was asked if he would travel to Chicago with his brother, he replied that he was reluctant to leave the fish he'd not yet caught. How I wish I'd pledged my rod to my own stream despite the debts and not fled to the metropolis.

The Reverend Maclean described his perished son as beautiful. I wonder if my father could say the same of me?

PISC: I enunciate an indubitable yes Ephemator. Now recall the most compelling sentence in the whole film.

'We can love completely without understanding.'

Ephemator, you weep. Come here and truly embrace your father.

PEDES: We've not ventured far and already I hear church bells.

PISC: But hark! That sound I hear is more melodious than any bells. 'Tis the glorious skylark. And my! My reading has beckoned him to grace this day for only last night before I fell to slumber I did alight on Pedestrian's sweet sonnet to the bird.

EPHEM: Well read it again dear friend. Match the melody and raise our spirits even higher.

PISC: It's here on page 9 of your little book Pedestrian if I can find it in my pocket.

I shall offer this recitation to the bird like incense.

The Skylark

Aloft her heaven song defies the probing eye,
Unseen in the panoramic sweep, her tiny heartbeat swelling.
Alone in bleated green I stop to peer and tingle,
Straining to spot a gossamer lightship, fixed and fluttering in the blue.
I bathe in song under the feathered belfry,
The tumbling chimes of infant bells,
Falling like ear-sweet snowflakes,
As bright as lambs in April,
As skittish as a gale-tossed kite,
To melt on my lips in a whistle,
As I fling up my cap in delight!

EPHEM: Delight indeed Sir! What a fanfare to send us on our way.

And here is the church, the bell ringers debouching from their practice for refreshment by its porch.

Good afternoon gentlemen!

BELLRINGERS (Chiming in chorus) Good afternoon!

ERNEST: (Conductor) Will you three ramblers join our band of ringers in a cup of tea? Our urn's bubbling away and we've got Bakewell Tart as well?

PISC: Thank you Sir. Your hospitality is generous and doth seem most appropriate to our needs. We've been travelling these three hours from London and our lips are dry.

My companions and I are grateful.

PEDES: Did I hear you say Bakewell Tart?

ERNEST: I did. A big one! My wife makes the finest Bakewell in the whole of Derbyshire.

BELLRINGERS: (Carilloning in concert). That's true. It takes our entire band to lift it!

ERNEST: So, what brings you to these parts? It's a lot quieter than London.

PEDES: I'm escorting these two gentlemen – er Ike and Charlie – on a sentimental journey over old paths. Years ago, they fished our lovely rivers.

ERNEST: You fished! Well, next to campanology, fishing is my favourite pastime. Blow me down.

Tell me – Charlie is it? – do you know the Dove?

Help yourself to sugar.

EPHEM: I do Sir. I once lived close by its banks near Hartington and I angled there as a boy.

ERNEST: Then you must have heard of your angling namesake Charles Cotton? I'm a huge fan. He's a legend round here and I still use some of the fly patterns he described all those years ago. They beat all the modern gimcracks. Why, some of the latest lures could scare the fish to death. He was also a poet and author you know and a bit of a lad by all accounts? I've got all of his first edition books and pamphlets. They cost me a damn fortune but I'm an avid collector of rare editions. I've got *The Wonders of the Peake*, a collection of topographical poems about this area; The *Compleat Gamester* about billiards, bowls and such like; *The Planters Guide*, a book on tree planting and *Scarronides* – a burlesque – it's mildly pornographic although it wouldn't turn a hair these days. And do you know, old Cotton once wrote an epitaph poem to one of his favourite prostitutes who he discreetly referred to as MH? It went something like this: '… he could pursue her memory with such a superstitious lust, that he could fumble with her dust.' What a wag. I told you he was a bit of a lad.

EPHEM: (Blushing) Mona, what a rare flower – but you've quoted one of his scurrilous minor works – yes, yes – Charles Cotton I've heard of him, I, I know him. But why haven't you got a copy of his most uplifting and enervating part work?

ERNEST: You mean *The Compleat Angler* by his friend and mentor – Izaak Walton. It's one of the best books ever written. Cotton contributed several chapters on fly-fishing in its fifth edition. But I couldn't afford a copy of even the tenth edition, not if I mortgaged the house. It's worth a bloody fortune! No, I have to content myself with a modern printing.

Both its authors are celebrated in the names of two local hotels – *The Izaak Walton* at the start of Dovedale and *The Charles Cotton* in Hartington. Fancy giving your name to a boozer! Isn't that the finest accolade?

And the last time I took my wife up to Dovedale for lunch they were serving a real ale named the *Izaak Walton.*

Fancy having a pint named after you. It beats an effigy in Westminster Abbey don't you think?

Have another slice of tart Ike.

Tell me, what sort of fishing do you like?

PISC: I spent most of my life pursuing what you call divers coarse fish in gentle ponds and rivers but on seeing a recent film, I'm totally converted to the art of the fly and to boisterous streams.

Have you seen *A River Runs Through It?*

ERNEST: Have I seen it! I've got the book, the film and the tee shirt. And what's even more exciting is that last year I joined a party of local lads on a lifetime's trip to Montana to fish the Big Blackfoot River. I never caught a trout quite as big as the one Brad Pitt wrestled with in the rapids but what a fantastic time we had. If you get the chance, go to America.

Here, I've an address card somewhere in my wallet. Take that and stay there. You'll have a great time.

But where are you staying tonight?

PEDES: I've booked us rooms at the *Black's Head and Green Man* in Ashbourne.

ERNEST: Oh, they'll look after you there. Tell them you met Ding Dong – my Sunday name's Ernie Bell – but even my wife calls me by my nickname – and you'll get great service.

Now then you band of Quasimodo look-alikes! We'd better be getting back to Tom, Dick and Harry and Little Ben before their little clappers get cold.

Cheerio! It's been great meeting you all gentlemen – now come along and shake all three hands like good ringers – and tight lines!

And before you go, please come into the church and enjoy
some of the finest carved bench ends in the country. Do have a look at them. They're worth seeing

PISC: We will and we thank you again Ding Dong and hope you enjoy your practice merrily on high!

And give our felicitations to your wife. The Bakewell Tart was most toothsome.

PEDES: Come on Ike and Charlie. Let's go inside and look at the bench ends. Do we need earmuffs?

ERNEST: Charlie! Charlie! I've just had a thought. Before I go, you might be able to help me? If you once lived round here, you must have heard of Ashbourne's Shrovetide Football Match? You have? Well, I'm writing a book on the subject and I'm attempting to prove that the football poem written by Cotton that refers to the anonymous two towns is actually about Ashbourne and Compton and our Shrovetide game? Do you know anything about it?

EPHEM: Let me cudgel my memory. Yes, it is about those two towns and I do remember writing it.

ERNEST: You do?

EPHEM: May I have the loan of a writing instrument and some paper and I'll end the confusion in a new version.

ERNEST: Here's a pen. How strange.

EPHEM: Strangest thing of all is that I remember it word for word.

There! The poem's amended now.

EPHEM: For the first time since I greeted you gentlemen in London, ten minutes have elapsed without a word. But please forgive me. I know the unchiding silence is a true mark of friendship. The disclosures by the bell ringer embarrassed and dismayed you both and, for a while, his recited words pummelled me like Paul's assailants in the alley.

The nib spills its ink and moves on but I know I'm forgiven.

I know atonement is not a scourging.

PISC: I saw you lighting a candle in the church. Was it for her? Was it for Mona?

EPHEM: You read my thoughts Master. The flame was for Mona and a dozen more. But know this, before my resurrection I would have needed a thousand candles to atone to them and both my wives.

You spoke only a few days ago about the power of heartfelt atonement and forgiveness and if ever that power was manifest, it manifests in me.

I'm shedding the shackles of ages on this Damascus road.

PISC: You now know that all words are expunged in our *mea culpas* and that God refills our inkpots to overflow.

But look, this helpful sign directs us along the Centenary Way.

Why is it so called Pedestrian?

PEDES: It's a 25-mile long route from Ilkeston to Ashbourne devised by the Derbyshire Footpaths Preservation Society to commemorate their centenary. It takes us from Brailsford and through the villages of Ednaston, Shirley, and Osmaston and on to the heart of Ashbourne.

Let's cross this field and we'll drop down to the very first of our Derbyshire brooks.

Brook: isn't that noun so melodic and full of murmured bliss? My Yorkshire equivalent is the rasping word beck. I think it most truculent and flinty.

I came walking here a few months ago and the banks were jostled with bluebells. Isn't it a delightful spot although you'll notice that the brook is much diminished?

Look right and you'll see that its flow has been intercepted to create a series of lakes. Over there on the bank. Those lads are fishing the Birch House Lakes – seven of them covering around twelve acres. And, like you Ephemator, they boast a Fishing Lodge. It's a meagre hut compared with the gem that you erected but catch the smell – they serve bacon sandwiches!

I fished on one of the lakes recently and had a fine day catching perch, roach, rudd and carp. Although I had a good haul, I couldn't compete with one angler who landed 116 pounds of fish in one session. He'd got amongst the tench.

PISC: Holy mackerel! By my computation that's in excess of 8 stones. St Andrew and his brothers would have been delighted with such a draught and they would have longed for the bacon sandwiches.

Quick! Cut me a sapling and pluck a twist of briar from yonder tangle Pedestrian – we're going a-fishing.

PEDES: Alas Master our planned itinerary does not permit a sojourn here. We must advance and walk on.

EPHEM: Verily gentlemen, it's so uplifting to gaze on my own shires once more. After the pavements of the city, these rolling hills really invigorate the spirit.

Oh! I remember as a small boy stripping naked one hot afternoon such as this and sprinting across the meadow with my friend Simon. Tumbling through dewy grass and gay flowers, we danced to the river and plunged headlong into an icy pool.

That same excitement now assails me, the urge to boyishness popping my buttons.

PEDES: It's not that warm!

EPHEM: No, we will keep our trousers fast.

But come. Lengthen your stride. I'm bursting with enervation.

I'll race you to the next stile!

PISC: Your chest is panting like a hot kettle Ephemator. Who won the race?

EPHEM: Pedestrian wears the laurels. He's too fleet for me.

PEDES: But you've the best excuse of all Ephemator. You've been asleep longer than Rip Van Winkle.

EPHEM: Who was he pray?

PEDES: Rip Van Winkle was a character in a short story by a nineteenth century author called Washington Irving. Mr Winkle fell asleep after drinking strong spirits with his neighbours and dozed for twenty years.

EPHEM: Nay, I had the same affliction after imbibing on your Kentish ale.

PEDES: Yes, you've already affirmed your preference for country liquors in your book. Didn't you remark that a man should not come from London to drink wine in the Peak?

EPHEM: I most certainly did.

PEDES: Well then, we'll shortly come to Ednaston and the *Yew Tree Inn*. Shall we call in and see if their brew merits your ancient praises? Fancy a pint of *Izaak Walton?*

PISC: There it is – just down the lane – a most attractive house.

In the time-honoured Yorkshire tradition imparted to me by my good friend Pedestrian … last man to the bar get's the drinks!

Trip him up Charlie!

PEDES: Hold on you two!

I'm closing! Phew! I've lost by a whisker. Oh, I must be getting old, pant, pant.

Now, what will you have?

PISC: Wilt thou cast thou eyes on the choice that greets us Ephemator? This week, Pedestrian's organisation and attention to detail have been faultless and exemplary but this array of aptly named country liquors bedazzles all before.

How planned you all this?

Study the colourful badges on the beer pumps. Those three ales must have been specially brewed to commemorate our peregrinations. But how?

Look! First in the line is *Doved Ale*, its badge showing two of the holiest birds in Christendom fluttering over the unmistakable Thorp Cloud. Next is *High Flyer* with an angler – it could be Paul Maclean – casting a fly in its centre. Our third choice of refreshment is *Holey Trinity.* And thither we are! The three of us are idling on a rock imbibing froth-rimmed six-hooped pots with our toes poking through our boots.

PEDES: So, you what'll you have?

PISC: Tarry Sir! How did you arrange this? It's beyond belief.

PEDES: Belief? Believe me Master this is none of my doing. I'm as gob smacked as you are. My surprise is total.

I have, as you say, been meticulous in the planning of our adventure but my simple talents and the skills of earth-born brewers could not encompass such a miracle.

I'm happy to reveal that throughout our tour, happenstance and serendipity have accompanied our every step. I've defined a rough itinerary but the fine and sumptuous details I've left to providence. Or should I say Godidence?

Let me tell you something profoundly wonderful and nourishing. After we went to bed last night, I had a dream. Before me was Our Lord with a golden chalice. He smiled at me sweetly and dipped His fingers into the holy cup, sprinkling droplets as He made the sign of the cross. Falling from heaven, the droplets spat and sizzled like beads of hot lead and were transformed into a rain of printer's type, a deluge of letters falling in unfailing order on the blank pages of a book.

The book was this *Complete Angler* through whose chapters we now thread.

So, my friends, what's it to be? *Doved Ale*, *High Flyer* or *Holey Trinity.*

EPHEM: These liquors are as surely blessed as the Last Supper wine but what will I choose? Yes, my predilection is for a jug of the brew that honours my beloved peak and dale.

PISC: And as a new convert to the art of fly-fishing I must drain the second choice.

PEDES: Mine must be a pint of *Holey Trinity.*

See, sat there in the middle of the two rogues? That's me, the good-looking one!

I do enjoy a good pint and this is superb. It has all the right attributes – taste, body and a good head – just like my wife.

A thick, creamy froth is important. It gives a unique dignity to a pint and the halo on this *Holey Trinity* betrays sainthood.

Are you watching? I'll plunge in with my tongue and enjoy a smacking salivation.

Hoogh! Hoogh! Ecstasy!

During my Sussex years, I had to contend with beer as flat as the doldrums calms, but this is the business.

What's yours like gentlemen.

EPHEM: It's the prince of all brews Pedestrian – the best I have ever tasted.

The roosted reality is that not everything in heaven is perfection. But it perplexes me, for if the Master Brewer can provide such nectar on earth why cannot he do it in heaven?

If the reputation of this triumvirate ascends aloft the unions will be alerted.

PISC: My liquor achieves similar excellence gentlemen. It must be the acme of the brewers' art. I've not quaffed better although methinks to drain the pot would slow me down to a crawl.

In the past, the old brewing monks would impress four smoking crosses on their barrels to attest to purity and strength. A hogshead of *High Flyer* would be branded to a cinder.

PEDES: Down to a crawl Piscator? If that's the case, sup up! Your speed over the ground at ninety years of age outpaces even our northern hares.

PISC: But remember Pedestrian I have new legs. I set out on this endeavour after having undergone what you would call a full service.

PEDES: If that's the case, bottoms up!

Come, on we go across the fields to Shirley. And there's another pub there!

But what's this? Our publican offers me duplicates of all three-beer pump badges as souvenirs.

Why thank you Sir.

PEDES: Already, we're in the fourth day of our adventure, the pointers on my pocket watch flying as fast as Mr Wells's Time Machine.

PISC: I'm unfamiliar with that name Sir.

PEDES: H G Wells was a recent author of science fiction Master. In one book, he presaged our flight to the moon and in another wrote of a fantastic journey backwards through time, the clock on his machine spinning its driver backwards and forwards through the centuries.

PISC: Verily, our presence here is not so fanciful!

PEDES: I've so little time and so much to ask you Master.
Let me venture the biggest question of them all.

We've already discoursed on the nature of happiness but why do we exist? What constitutes a fruitful life?

PISC: You probe me with two questions Sir. Let me conjure faithful replies.

As I have insisted before, you are to take notice that I cannot add anything to the teachings of all the philosophers, theologians, metaphysicians, enlightened poets and holy men who with lowly feet have strode as the Colossus on this blessed Earth. Their nuggets abound for the finding and polishing Sir.

Find them.

Truly, my friend, a river does run through our existence and it gushes from one source, the springing of its issue chuckling with The Word. We need to return to the fountainhead to find it.

Go there, follow the stream, and all the world's religions – their rites and rituals – merge into one, the holy books and icons, the beliefs and recitations, the traditions and ceremonies, the bigotries, animosities and intolerance evaporating like a shower in the sun.

Go there and find the rainbow and your first question is answered.

But what's the nub of our purpose and a meaningful existence? I'll answer thus.

Our simple duty as human beings is to contribute to life, our passing conferring a net and honest gain, each according to his gifts and talents. In doing this, it is our joyful duty to revere and relish the riches of the world, always filling our cups half full and sharing as we go.

The mind of man is lured to ever more complex and labyrinthine places Pedestrian but you sweet friend do clutch a torch that shineth bright.

PEDES: Me Master? How can that be?

PISC: Before I met you in Winchester, I did enquire as to your character and nature, some of your friends smiling in the admission that you, and I quote, 'didn't do complications.'

You radiate contentment with what you have in the moment Sir. It's a lesson to which all the improvers and modernisers should take heed, because all their fevered probings will lead nowhere else but to that one true source.

And while I offer these humble thoughts I'll add a comment that really makes me vexed.

PEDES: You vexed Master!

PISC: Yes, indeed!

All your religions, and my former following too, doth impose strict routes to salvation. Follow their guideposts, chant their psalms and incantations, offer rare sacrifices and debase yourselves and you shall attain the highest stations. What poppycock!

PEDES: Strong language Master!

PEDES: It's tommyrot! The only route to salvation is through the proper steer of conscience. And what of the men and women who lived and died before the birth of all the rules and prescriptions? What pray of all the fellows who trod the virgin soil 500, 5000, nay 50,000 years past? Are they, for the lack of a book and candle to be condemned for evermore?

It's flap-doodle I tell you!

PEDES: Have you heard these fulminations Ephemator? It's as well I've been recording the speech on my pocket Dictaphone, so that I may recover every word and commit them to this page.

If High Flyer lubricates the chords of such wisdom, elegance and hot vituperation, I'll order twenty hogsheads full.

But talking of hogsheads, at the end of this wonderful holly hedge is the village of Shirley and another pub.

Here it is, the *Saracen's Head*. Shall we call in for more refreshment? What will we find inside?

PISC: Nothing please my friend for we press on to our lodgings in Ashbourne lest you have to wheel me thither in a barrow.

PEDES: But Master, curiosity constrains me. I must cross the threshold to see if the Royal Victualler has repeated his miracle.

Please, just for a few moments, wait for me under this swinging sign as I check the fountainhead.

EPHEM: Surely the magic cannot be repeated?

PISC: In this miraculous week, I rule out nothing, surprise and enchantment following us every day. Pedestrian is a lightening rod for delights and expectations.

Yes, behold through yonder window, he speaks in jolly animation with the landlord. And the man pulls three draughts, our Pedestrian carrying three tiny glasses on a tray.

What have you there dear Sir?

PEDES: What have I here? Why, I've tasting samples of yet another batch of holy brews.

For you Piscator. Praise the Lord and raise your glass to *The River Sow*. And examine this gifted pump badge. That's you Sir and old Silas beside you looking through your spyglass!

And for you Ephemator, a small drop of *Pike Pool*, drink up, drink up! And on your pump badge, an image of you clambering up the stone to retrieve your fly.

As for me gentlemen, a dribble of *The Compleat Tangler,* my badge showing yours truly in dazed and dizzy stupefaction with a hive of bees and a knotted fishing line and float and hook around my ears.

Doesn't Our Lord have a wicked sense of humour?

Let's hope he's not reprised his trick at every pub from here to Hartington. There's over a dozen in Ashbourne alone. If we call in every one, you'll have to carry me out in a coffin.

PISC: And then we must float you to heaven!

PEDES: See the next footpath sign? We continue now on what's known as the Bonnie Prince Charlie Walk. It was created a few years ago to remember the 200th anniversary of Charles Edward Stuart's invasion of England in 1745. He was a Scot with a legitimate claim to the English crown. But it all ended in tears. He only got as far as Derby and retreated to Ashbourne where he stayed the night before fleeing back to Scotland.

PISC: And I think I'm blessed having a beer named after me.

When I return next week, I'll proposition The Holy Ordnance Survey and we'll have a walk named after you Pedestrian.

PEDES: No need. They're all named after me Master. They're all pedestrian routes.

EPHEM: This place looks strangely familiar. If I ventured a name, would I be wide of the mark in thinking I tread the demesne of Osmaston Park? Long ago, I think I came here once. I have a very vague recall of a forge by a lake. Maybe Simon brought me here?

PEDES: It's that very same Osmaston Park Sir. We'll drop down now through the trees on a track to a lake. You may be surprised at what we find.

EPHEM: There it is Pedestrian! My, it's just as I remember it and although the anvil is cold and silent, the waterfall tumbles on.

On first encounter, I thought this one of the most picturesque scenes in the whole of Derbyshire.

PEDES: When I first saw it a few months ago, I was similarly captivated. It's so attractive even in dereliction and seems to have been used last as a sawmill. When I poked my head through its cobwebbed windows and examined the rusting bones of its industry, I saw in my minds eye a halcyon home, my imagination running riot with thundering hammers and paint brushes galore and me leading my blindfolded wife to its door. And in the dream, I'd already planted saxifrage and edelweiss around the falls!

EPHEM: It would make a fine home. Keep its vision safe like a prized jewel and the reality will be so Pedestrian.

PEDES: It's a place for lingering but we continue upwards to the village of Osmaston where we'll tiptoe past the *Shoulder of Mutton.*

But it seems we have feathered company.

PISC: I have never witnessed such an abundance of pheasants. What handsome but artless birds. How they scuttle and run.

PEDES: Alas, they're all doomed Master. They'll face raking twin barrels and squalls of lead once the shooting season begins in the autumn. The birds are specially reared for the slaughter. It really saddens me. In flight they are as ungainly and sluggish as peacocks. I really think I could knock them from the sky with a schoolboy's catapult or a slingshot but they're brought down with fusillades from guns sometimes costing thousands of pounds.

Years ago I took a job as a beater and watched with some disgust as several short-sighted, near crippled gentlemen were propped up with their guns to await the arrival of the birds. Beating sticks and hollering, we beaters crashed through the wood, pheasants and other terrified game exploding to flight. Seeing some of the birds cowering in the brush, I lifted my feet, urged them to silence and made detours around them through the wood. But it made no difference and the carnage was awful. The old boys couldn't miss. I wouldn't have minded so much if the carcases had fed hungry families but at the end of the shoot, there they lay, scores of unwanted pheasants and partridge in the back of a van with their gorgeous heads lolloping, beads of blood dripping from their beaks. Not one of the guns could be bothered to take them home for the onerous task of plucking and gutting.

Any caring soul who has ever examined the behaviour of a pheasant closely will tell you that at the sight of man the birds exhibit abject fear and panic akin to some soldier in the First World war trenches who, on hearing the thunder of the guns, involuntarily evacuated his bowels. In terror, the birds' do the same even with unarmed walkers like us, the ancestral fear of been blown dismembered from the sky twitching every feather.

As you might have guessed, I dislike guns and hunting.

In the old days there was a certain dignity about a hunter who with skill and daring tackled a wild animal to bring meat to the table. Some beasts', damn it, could fight back! Now though it's just senseless mayhem.

I'm off again matching your vexation Master. Pardon my passion.

EPHEM: Well voiced Pedestrian! You've enough fire in your belly to match the roar of Mons Meg. The Master and I concur with your opinions.

PISC: We certainly do. It's good that a man has passion. On this journey, a truly repentant Ephemator has been forgiven for his profligacy and wild ways and I too have been granted similar absolution for my vehement attacks on the poor otter. We stand corrected, entrained in new paradigms and at one with you Pedestrian. Run on noble birds!

But you are pensive and reflective Sir. A penny for your thoughts.

PEDES: Your words dislodge a clot of conscience Master. It sticks in my throat like a fur-ball in the craw of a daft owl and chokes me to admission.

PISC: What could trouble you so? You are to know that you are amongst true friends and that you too may vomit this conscience to forgiveness.

PEDES: I, I, lied to you Master.

PISC: You lied to me?

PEDES: I lied to you about the pike you caught in the River Lea for you see, my concern for wild creatures embraces not only pheasants. I'm afraid it's slowly extending to everything that flies and swims.

Out of compassion, I told 41 to return the pike to the river. I'm afraid it's not at the taxidermists.

Do forgive me for misleading you.

PISC: If that's the sum of your admission Pedestrian, cough and sing like a nightingale. You are a sweet bird!

PEDES: That's not the whole story Master. Before I wafted his gills and pointed the fish upstream to freedom, I took his photograph. In fact, I took several photographs. My plan is this. My daughter has an incredible talent for creating magical forms from folded and sculpted papers. She recently fashioned a life-sized peacock, commissioned by a London fine paper company to advertise the printing of a richly adorned book of translation – *The Rubaiyat of Omar Kyam*. This book of metaphysical poems will have the tooled image of a peacock on its cover. Its contents would appeal to you Ephemator. Written in the 12th century by a Persian poet, mathematician and astronomer, the book of around one thousand poems has been extensively translated in recent centuries. I've read some of the renditions, one particular poem uncannily echoing the words you uttered not an hour ago.

> *The moving finger writes and having writ moves on.*
> *Nor all thy piety nor wit, shall lure it back to cancel half a line,*
> *nor all thy tears wash out a word of its.*

But I mightily digress. The pike. I'll have my daughter create a simulacrum of the fish in weedy ambuscade to reside in a glass case, your signature and imprint Piscator and details of its capture appearing in gold letters on a supporting silver plinth. And all to be paid for with money donated by a sponsor. I must tell him! Once crafted, the fish will be sold at a top London auction house, the proceeds going along with our match day winnings to a worthy cause.

PISC/EPHEM:(In unison) What a splendid idea Pedestrian! You really are inspired.

PEDES: Well, if I'm forgiven the subterfuge let's march smartly on past the unnamed licensed premises – platoon eyes left! – saluting the noble church in thanksgiving for our abstemious resolve.

No, we're not thirsty are we men?

PISC: We could cross the Sahara and be content with a dry sponge couldn't we Ephemator?

EPHEM: We could Master.

PEDES: We're not far from my lovely Ashbourne now. First we pass through this caravan park and drop down to the busy A52 road. I'll escort you across into an estate of modern houses.

PISC: You speak of the town warmly as your own Pedestrian. Do you reside there?

PEDES: No Master. I currently live in the luxurious apartment of a manor house in the village of Bradbourne some six or so miles northeast of the town. From my windows I can scan the White Peak and my playground of hills and rivers. I lay in my bed of a morning supping tea and watching the cows and sheep grazing. It's a most invigorating occupation for a man of sixty-five.

PISC: Ye Gods! Did you hear that Ephemator? Our agile guide is sixty-five. I would never have fathomed it. He looks younger than you.

PEDES: I hasten to remind you Sir that you're ninety and although you're old enough to be my dad we look of an age.

PISC: But you forget Pedestrian, and I'll tell you again, that I've had the benefit of what you would call in modern parlance – I overheard the conversation of the chambermaid in the *Trysting Tree Hotel* – of a divine makeover.

PEDES: Well, it's good to be fit and active and to rejoice at being so. Age is relative. On cold, damp mornings, I do enjoy snuggling under my duvet with my tea and toast – watch the crumbs darling – but when the sun shines I'm into my boots in one bound and off across the meadow to pick flowers or mushrooms for my sweetheart. From a distance, my angel smiles sweetly and waves as I collect posies and breakfast. It's such a wonderful life.

It's a pity that our short time together won't permit a detour to my home at Bryn Hall. My wife makes fabulous scones every bit as good as Mrs Bell's Bakewell Tarts. She was given the recipe by a lady who ran a celebrated teashop in Sussex.

EPHEM: We cannot taste but we can savour Master! Tell me Pedestrian; the emporium of which you speak, is it the one eulogised in your poem *Cottage Tea*? It is? Verily, we shall feast upon the words.

Your little book – I have it in my pocket. Page, page, page 29. Here it is.

Cottage Tea

Rushing through the woods, like prospectors sniffing out the mother-load.
'Last one pays!' her wake-washed shout, an impish declaration.

Fresh baked, sultana bulged and dusted,
The unctuous jam and cream,
With trembling palette knives,
To daub in sticky admiration.

Our cottage tea for two entrayed,
Oh eager salivation!
Swelling lips, to suck, to press,
To bite in drooling exultation!

And what about this note affixed at the bottom? *Written on a serviette after yet another short encounter with the best scones in the kingdom at the tea garden in Jevington, East Sussex … I paid… again.*

Is your beloved wife also of a Yorkshire persuasion?

PEDES: No Ephemator, she's German by birth although the citizens of that country also have a habit of forgetting their purses.

PISC: All this drooling exultation is exciting my digestive juices gentlemen.

Is it much further?

PEDES: No Master. We'll shortly leave this estate and arrive at the top of Old Hill, re-uniting with the route our friend took all those years ago.

I see you quicken your stride Ephemator. You've the smell of the old peaks in your nostrils. Not long to tarry now. A few steps more. From the top of Old Hill and north to Paradise! There! What say you?

EPHEM: I feel like throwing my cap in the air and sounding Gabriel's horn. Humbled and ecstatic, I feel like rushing down to yonder church and lighting twin candles in atonement and thanksgiving.

PEDES: From this summit, we plunge downwards into Ashbourne. Apart from the cave on your left, there's very little to recognise hereabouts but you'll soon see a bridge over a brook, Dig Street delivering us to our old coaching inn – *The Black's Head and Green Man* – where we'll spend the night.

EPHEM: I marvel at being able to tread these streets once more. And look Master! Peer down from this bridge and rejoice at the sight of my own Henmore.

PEDES: Turn right at the corner gentlemen and stop under the wooden sign that spans the road, the central mask of a black man marking our journey's end for today.

When you came before Sir, you stopped at the *Talbot* and enjoyed a glass of ale on horseback. That alehouse has long since disappeared – it was demolished in 1786 – but *The Black's Head* is a fine successor and you'll be comfortable here.

Our names will be added to a distinguished guest list gentlemen. See that plaque on the wall? It commemorates the visit of James Boswell who stayed here in 1777. Like you Master he was a biographer. His book about Samuel Johnson, who is arguably the most distinguished man of letters in English history, is claimed to be the most famous single work of biographical art in the whole of literature.

I must read it.

Now, without more fanfare, I'll check us in and you can both relax in your rooms for a few hours.

I know you're hungry gentlemen. I'll have a tray of refreshments sent up to tie you over until we eat this evening.

Bye for now … I'll meet you in the bar at 7 o'clock sharp!

FOURTH DAY

CHAPTER FOUR

Up'ards and down'ards

Wednesday. The Feast of St Goar. Evening. The Green Man and *Black's Head Hotel, Ashbourne.*

PEDES: Good evening gentlemen! I trust you enjoyed your afternoon teas? It seemed cruel to excite your drooling and deny you the mother load.

EPHEM: Thank you, the scones were delicious were they not Master? And I'll tell you this; if your wife bakes a finer bun you had better rewrite your poem.

PISC: Yes, the scones were wonderful Pedestrian but I hope I have capacity for my evening repast. All that cream!

PEDES: Speaking of cream, look at the head on that! It's an Irish stout we call Guinness.

PISC: I'll have one of those.

EPHEM: And me also.

PEDES: Please take menus gentlemen and let me know your choices. After all that travelling, I'm ravenous and I think I'll have the rib eye steak with lashings of chips and vegetables.

PISC: Me too please.

EPHEM: And me also kind Sir.

PEDES: It's steaks all round then. While I'm at the bar, look at the framed photographs over there. They show an event that's brought Ashbourne international fame. You referred to it earlier Ephemator in your conversation with Ernie Bell.

EPHEM: Thank you gracious Pedestrian. My, it's such a stygian brew. I've been studying the photographs and I'm amazed. Those astonishing images. After all these centuries, the Shrovetide Football Match survives. Ernie was right. I did write a poem about the match but there were then two distinct halves to this town – Ashbourne and Compton – constrained by the Henmore Brook. T'was the division that created the rivalry. The pictures resurrect memories of mine and Simon's own involvement as young boys, the local apothecaries doing great trade in balms and embrocations in the mending of broken fingers and torn ears. Such was our appearance on returning to Beresford Hall after one particularly fevered game, that I had to convince father that we'd been tossed by a bull!

PEDES: I've a similar recall of the match I attended this very year. I was keen to participate, realising that the Ashbourne game is the only such event surviving in England.

PISC: Tell us about it Pedestrian.

PEDES: A newcomer to this area, I journeyed from Bradbourne by bus. Approaching the town, I wondered if normally genteel Ashbourne had suffered an overnight air raid or a mass burglary such was the plethora of boarded up and plank-protected shops and offices. But no, the casements were intact, one resident who ducked into a shop to buy his daily newspaper explaining that the timbers were intended to prevent damage that in previous years had kept local glaziers busy for weeks. Bemused, I went into a hotel, this very hotel. Cleared of its tables and chairs, it seethed with customers all chatting about the forthcoming match between the *Up'ards* and *Down'ards*, the contest between local factions tracing its origins, they explained, to a dispute lasting 700 years. 'I once touched the ball,' boasted a twenty stone beast in a rugby shirt, paint-spattered trousers and steel toe-capped boots. 'No lad,' he added guffawing at my modest frame, smart winter attire and training shoes. 'There's no rules. You have to get the ball between the goals set three miles apart. It sometimes ends up in the brook. You'll be far too warm in that lot despite the snow. It's baking hot inside the maul. It's just a mass of bodies.'

As two o'clock approached, I joined the exodus to the purpose built rostrum where the ball was 'turned up', a plaque telling me that I was following in royal footsteps, His Royal Highness the Prince of Wales – later King Edward VIII – taking part in the proceedings in 1928 and getting a bloody nose for his troubles.

Following a warning not to enter any graveyard or old folks home, *Auld Lang's Ayne* and the *National Anthem* were sung and the ball was tossed aloft. I never saw it again.

Lost in a throng of around 300 heaving and grunting bodies, suffocating on a steamy cocktail of sweat, testosterone and beer fumes, I gasped for breath and was carried along helplessly like a ping pong ball on a raging tide of men, the tornado of twisting, human flesh flattening flower beds, tearing up lawns and demolishing lamp standards, the demoniacal shouts of at least 10,000 spectators urging us on.

Stop laughing so loudly gentlemen or you'll both have hernias! And your surfeit of cream will turn to butter!

Then the road was closed by the police, the knot surging forth to test the shop defences. With my feet off the ground, I felt like a toad at a hippopotami convention and struggled to get free, this 10 stone pip finally being squeezed out as the melee tumbled into the Henmore Brook, one young man making off with the ball and entering an underground culvert. Three hours later, with no more casualties than one would expect at a Leeds United versus Millwall football match, a goal was scored and the pubs' were re-opened in triumph. Still trembling but with my limbs intact, I slinked back on the bus and went to bed.

PISC: Bravo Pedestrian! What a tale and you pull up your trouser leg to reveal the scars of combat. What a fellow you are. I salute you in this fine ale.

M-mm-mm. It tastes like an admixture of burnt cork and straw but it's agreeably palatable.

He was brave was he not Ephemator? You were a colt but he was –

PEDES: A rather shrunken carthorse Sir! But it was an experience not to be missed.

So here we are Ephemator in Ashbourne the gateway to your beloved Dovedale. In anticipation of our visit, I've been touring the Dove's length. And what a tour! Last month I set out to discover its source. For us brothers of the angle, it's our watery Jerusalem.

EPHEM: You went to Axe Head? You will remember it Master. There by the roadside, our infant river gurgling forth from a cistern carved with our entwined initials.

PEDES: Yes, I went there and had some difficulty finding the spot. Until, until, I heard a buzzard circling overhead. It appeared like the nativity star and I found the source babbling still, thick alder and willow clothing its early rushing. In recalling the time I went as a pilgrim to the shrine of Bernadette in the French town of Lourdes, I took out my bottle and filled it full of water. I have the bottle here in my pocket. As my priest bedaubed the Easter chrism of old, I should sign your brows with its holy drops … *in nomine partris et filii et spiritus sancti.* Or should I save it to sweeten our after dinner whisky? Either way, we're all well blessed.

After leaving the Dove's source, as it was a hot day, I called in at the nearby *Travellers Rest* to quench my thirst and again something extraordinary happened in a long series of events that have made the compilation of this book such an enormous thrill and pleasure. I took a glass of ginger beer and settled on a stool opposite the bar, a small library of books behind me catching my eye. I reached out with a random touch and pulled forth a book.

Have a guess what it was Master?

PISC: I've no inkling Pedestrian. Pray relieve our suspense.

PEDES: It was *No Man is an Island – A Selection of the Prose of John Donne.* I opened it and miraculously it fell open at a page showing an engraving of Donne's friend and biographer. He was sat there taking his rest under a tree with rod and landing net. It was you Master!

PISC: I'm replete, that was a fine plate of meat, its sinews almost matching the fibre of this black brew.

PEDES: Would you like a refill Sir?

PISC: Thank you no. And I'll decline your offer of a pudding. I may though, with your good grace, partake of a cup of coffee and dram of the whisky you spoke of.

EPHEM: You might indulge me also Pedestrian.

Yet again, he fusses and frets over our wellbeing Master. Look at him discussing our needs with the pot man. From the first moment of our acquaintance, he's devoted all his energies to the success of our precious contract. But if I may repeat the question I posed of you yesterday: are you satisfied with our enterprise?

PISC: I am so my friend. Methinks, I'm more than satisfied. I set out last Sunday with some misgivings and not a little trepidation but this whole journey has already been thoroughly enjoyable and fulfilling and I do feel that our compact with Our Saviour is being admirably met. Our ancient book will indeed have new wings.

PEDES: There you are gentlemen, a snort of *Glen Morangie*, one of the finest malts to come out of Scotland. And may I suggest a little splash of this holy water in each glass.

EPHEM: Ah sweet Dove. I can touch and taste it and I can almost smell its wider course.

PEDES: Well, it's just over yonder hill.

EPHEM: Will it greet us soon? What have you got in store for us on the morrow?

PEDES: I'm afraid you'll have to tarry yet one more day before you greet your precious glides. But don't be dismayed. This is Cotton country and my action-packed itinerary seeks to fill every second with rich associations with your family name. There'll be grand reunions to make your head spin!

But we'll not take your old route. You once climbed away from Ashbourne north on the old Buxton road but it's now much too busy with quarry traffic. You'd not travel far before your bones would be ground down for motorway ballast! Nor will we leave that road and take the track to Hanson Toot and Milldale. No. You'll be overjoyed to hear my friend that we can now walk the entire length of Dove Dale, Mill Dale, Wolfscote Dale and Beresford Dale from the village of Thorpe to Hartington. We won't miss a single yard of the river. How exciting is that?

First though, we'll walk from here to Tissington, visiting Fenny Bentley along the way. And we'll take a delightful route unknown in your time. We'll amble along the Tissington Trail. It follows the track of an abandoned railway line that once ran from Ashbourne to Buxton. The line was opened in 1899 and in its hey day it carried express trains from Manchester to London. It was finally closed in the 1960's and opened as a cycle track and footpath in 1991.

It's so quiet and peaceful. You'll absolutely love it.

EPHEM: I'll have a restless might in fevered expectation.

PEDES: No, you must sleep well for we've a fair hike before us tomorrow although we can rest in the afternoon.

Now, I must take leave of you gentlemen and bid you a good night for my head is nodding and I risk drowning in my own drink.

Sleep well my friends.

EPHEM/PISC (together) Sleep well Pedestrian. Good night.

EPHEM: Despite the effects of this sedative noggin, I fear excitement shall keep the shutters of sleep full wide.

Do you know Master, there's a framed paper in my room. It smokes with memories of my old home.

PISC: What is its nature pray?

EPHEM: It advertises the auction sale of Beresford Hall in 1825 to be conducted in this very hotel. And it mentions you and I.

BERESFORD HALL, STAFFORDSHIRE

(FORMERLY THE RESIDENCE OF CHARLES COTTON, Esq.)

TO BE SOLD BY AUCTION

BY

MR. NICHOLSON

ON WEDNESDAY, THE 10TH DAY OF AUGUST NEXT, 1825,

AT THE HOUSE OF MR WOOD, "THE GREEN MAN," IN ASHBOURNE,

AT TWO O'CLOCK IN THE AFTERNOON, –

All that the Manor or reputed Manor of Beresford, in the County of Stafford, consisting of an Ancient Mansion or Hall House, Rookery &c. &c., and near 90 Acres of Land, on the River Dove, which forms the eastern boundary of the property; the rocks and the whole of the romantic scenery of this property are well clothed with both ancient and young timber; and it is well known to the public, not only for its very great and picturesque beauty, but also from its having been the favourite residence and place of retirement of Mr. COTTON, and of his friend, IZAAK WALTON;

CONSISTING OF

No.	*A.*	*R.*	*P.*
1.—The Mansion House, Garden and small Plot on the north side	0	2	10
2.—Orchard..	2	3	18
3.—Kitchen, Garden, 7c.	3	1	18
4.—Near Cow Close	4	1	11
5.—Far ditto	3	1	5
6.—Near Hog's Meadow	12	0	25
7.—Paddock	12	2	27
8.—Oxhays	7	2	26
9.—Horse Shoe	12	1	1
10.—Far Hog's Meadow	12	3	31
11.—Plantation	0	14	1
12.—Plantation	3	0	15
13.—The Hill Side, 7c.	8	4	10
14.—Plantation	0	0	12
15.—The Heathy Closes	10	0	0
16.—The Smedley Hole	2	0	0
17.—Cottage and Croft at Archer Moor	0	2	0
18.—Ditto, Beresford Lane, about	0	1	0
Together	85	3	0

And making (with the River) near 90 Acres in the whole, about 70 Acres of which are excellent Dairy Land.

FIFTH DAY

CHAPTER ONE

On the Tissington Trail

Thursday. The Feast of St Pantaenus. Morning. Ashbourne High Street.

PEDES: Well, if your both ready, off we go. Yet again we're honoured with sunshine. My toes are dancing in anticipation of another fine day.

But before we leave this town gentlemen, I should like to take you along Church Street to visit St Oswald's. It's not far out of our way.

You'll perhaps remember this part of Ashbourne Ephemator? The Queen Elizabeth Grammar School to your right. It was built in 1585 with proceeds from the will of a local knight Sir Thomas Cockayne. I must tell you an amusing story about it. You remember last night when I spoke about Samuel Johnson being the most distinguished man of letters in English history? Well, he once applied for the post of Under Master at yonder school and was turned down!

And here's Ashbourne's magnificent church. It has many treasures that will tug the ancestral strings Ephemator and one more than must catch both your hearts. Come, let's go inside.

This is the chapel I've brought you to see. It's called the Cockayne or sometimes the Boothby Chapel. Isn't it serenely beautiful? It also contains memorials to the Bradbourne family.

I believe some of these tombs honour distant relatives of yours Ephemator?

EPHEM: That's so Pedestrian. My Beresford blood mingles with that of the Cockayne's. I recall seeing some of these sarcophagi before.

PEDES: Look at this Sir. It will really re-ignite your interest. The inscription tells us that it's the tomb of another Sir Thomas Cockayne. Known as 'The Magnificent', he died in April 1537 and was knighted after the siege of Tourney. He was also present at the Field of the Cloth of Gold. And see here at the bottom right hand corner – a rhyming epitaph. It could well be the earliest in existence.

All these monuments are works of art but none of them can compare with the sculpture in the corner.

Come Master, let me show you a tribute to a young girl that may raise a tear. People from all over the world visit Ashbourne just to see the effigy of Penelope Boothby.

A prodigy who could speak four languages, little Penelope was adored by her family but she died before her sixth birthday. Her devoted parents were crushed by the tragedy and from the day of her demise, such was their grief, that neither uttered another word to each other, the distraught father seeking solace in emigration.

PISC: The exquisite delicacy and beauty of this sculpture and the tragic tale of its begetting would tug at any parents heartstrings. My beloved first wife Rachel and I were blessed with six sons and one daughter but the fluxes and vile vapours of London claimed them all in infancy. All humanity weeps for the death of innocent infants like this poor Penelope. Thankfully, I was blessed to remarry my beloved Ann and we had three children, by the grace of God, my daughter Anne and my last born son Issac surviving.

The sight of this virginal marble compels a prayer and a touching. Those tiny toes have been polished by a thousand fingers.

EPHEM: Master, Master, over here. I've something to show you.

I found this card on the plinth of one of the Bradbourne tombs. The man referred to here must be related to the noble family who gave their name to Bradbourne village?

Now lo! Here is the cause you spoke of Pedestrian on the Feast of St Athanasius. Our £50's may have found a home.

May I read the narrative about John Bradburne?

Third Order Franciscan, mystic, poet and friend of lepers. Born in England in 1921, he served with the Ghurkhas in Malaya and Burma during World War II. A Pauline-like conversion led him to become a pilgrim seeker, first with the Benedictines and then with the Carthusians although he remained a layman to the end. His search for God's will led him through England, Europe and the Holy Land mostly on foot. In 1962 he went to 'seek a cave' in Zimbabwe. Instead he found Mutemwa Leprosy Settlement. There he tended a flock of 80 leprosy patients with loving care, laying down his life for them on September 5th 1979.

At his funeral, a pool of blood was seen beneath his coffin. On opening it, there was no evidence of where the blood had come from. However, an oversight was revealed: John had not been clothed in the habit of St Francis as is the privilege of members of the Third Order and had been John's wish. The habit was found and John was clothed in it.

Since his death, there have been many signs of his sanctity: reports of miracles, claims of cures as well as many answers to prayer. More important, many have turned to God through John's extraordinary example.

And at the bottom of the card is one of John's short poems entitled *Strange Vagabond*.

God's love within you is your native land.
So search none other, never more depart.
For you are homeless save God keeps your heart.

And there's information about donations. I think we've found our worthy cause gentlemen.

PISC: 'Tis so. And God willing, the funds from the sale of your paper pike will also swell the coffers.

What say you Pedestrian?

PEDES: If I'd arranged to put that stack of cards there myself, I couldn't be more pleased. Yes, we've found our cause.

And feel: the cards still have the printers dew on them. I wonder who put them there?

PEDES: Here's another riddle for you both. My, how I like to keep you on your toes! Where my friends is the Tissington Trail?

We're back on Church Street and it's only feet away. But where is it?

PISC: I look around but I'm flummoxed Sir.

EPHEM: I too am cumbumbled.

PEDES: It's beneath your feet! It's in a tunnel! Follow me to its entrance.

We go right here and right again down the steps and voila! The Tissington Trail!

PISC: The brickwork is most imposing, its creators leaving a wondrous arch.

EPHEM: But I hear the sound of panting steel.

PISC: Don't be alarmed my friend. It's merely the good converters of this route who want to provide authenticity. The noise of the old steam engines is played through loudspeakers on the walls.

EPHEM: For a moment, I almost turned in flight.

PEDES: Relax Sir and enjoy this walk. Apart from the odd bicycle and their tinkling bells, there'll be nothing to disturb you all the way of our 3½ miles to Tissington. You could almost saunter along with your eyes shut and shuffle along in carpet slippers.

And talking of that, why don't you link arms with the Master and I and shut your peepers tight? We'll guide you along until we arrive at a sight that'll make your irises pop.

What great fun!

I used to do this with my mother and father and found it magical.

Now, open them!

We're now stood on a bridge over the delectable Bradbourne Brook. You must have fished its waters as a boy?

EPHEM: Yes, yes! I sometimes stayed in Bentley Old Hall not far from here, this brook almost passing its door. Does the hall still stand? I hesitate to venture such a question.

PISC: It still stands and I'll have a treat for you in a mile or so. We'll take a short detour off this track and wander over fields, crossing the Wash Brook towards Fenny Bentley where you may see what remains of the old place for yourself. And we'll call in at St Edmund's Church and recall your lineage, bringing the story of your family fully up to date.

Surprised?

EPHEM: Surprised, enchanted and not a little humbled Sir.

PISC: You were correct in saying that this is Cotton country Pedestrian. When I came here last, there was not a rustic that omitted to tip his hat or offer a toothsome tithe to this man.

It's meet that he's back in his own country with two boon friends.

Fancy Ephemator, we now walk where hundreds of tons of fiery dragons once plied. Rushing volcanoes, they must have lit up the countryside?

PEDES: Lit up! Lit up! Yes, I remember such steam engines from my childhood Master. They were living, breathing beasts with throbbing shafts and pistons and thundering wheels, clouds of billowing, spark-ladened smoke and steam enveloping and choking us as they sped by. Out of school, spotting them and recording their details in our books was our principle entertainment and it cost nothing. Dozens of us urchins in short pants would congregate in railway stations and marshalling yards to await their arrival. Sometimes, we knew what type of engine approached by the sound of its chimney emissions alone. We'd stand there waving, shouting and cheering on bridges and platforms. It was a joyous thing, not unlike the celebrations afforded to the return of conquering heroes. To us, they were all heroes. Nearly sixty years on, I can give you all their names – yes, quite a number of the engines had romantic names – polished plates celebrating birds, racehorses, beauty spots, halls and castles, countries and book titles. But whatever happened to my own *Shotover, Harvester* and *The Braes of Derwent*? They were all scrapped. Nowadays, enthusiasts have preserved a few lines and engines for posterity but the rest are just pieces of grit in the eye and happy memories.

PISC: But you explained Pedestrian that this line was removed of the leviathans only some fifty years past. If that's so how has nature taken what was surely a scar and healed it so completely?

Just listen to the birdsong in this dell and see the profusion of wild flowers.

PEDES: Whatever man does to the earth, nature takes it back good or bad and gives it new clothes. Is that not so Master? When the railway builders subjugated this landscape with their drills and explosives, little did they realise that they were ultimately creating a haven for wildlife and walkers like us.

On a more philosophical and universal note, I'm content in the knowledge that whatever vile injuries and pollutions we inflict on our planet home – and we've spoken about global warming and de-forestation long into the night – that all will be rendered and reused in the cataclysmic crucible that is our ultimate fate.

PISC: You speak wisely Sir, all profligate peoples needing to realise that nature is blind and uncaring. Man neither creates nor destroys and only can only temporarily alter this world. If he fails in his stewardship of this sweet earth, he will not subtract an atom from the fire-hot mix that begot the planet. Every eternal particle will be reused and reborn to another more caring race.

EPHEM: Will you desist my friends? Can you put your philosophising aside for a while? All this talk of belching smoke and fire is putting the linnet out of tune.

PEDES: Please! Just one more reference to sparks and steams trains! And I promise it will be light-hearted Ephemator and most heart-warming for you Master.

You will recall that in your will, you bequeathed Halfhead Farm in Staffordshire to you son Issac. That bequest, you may remember, was made with a condition attached. And it was this. If Issac didn't marry before his 41st birthday, the farm would be transferred to the corporation of Stafford and money from its rent would be used to succour the poor people of the town. Well, I can tell you that bachelor Issac never did tie the knot, the condition coming into force in 1694. With the proceeds from the rents, each year, two boys from impoverished families were apprenticed to a trade and in addition, a selected maid was given £1 to celebrate her wedding day. In addition, £5 10s was allocated to buy winter coal for the needy.

Aren't you wonderfully gratified Master?

PISC: I am a little disappointed that Issac never wed but incredibly gratified that my legacy profited the citizens of Stafford town. But you mentioned a connection with steam trains Sir. You prevaricate, or all that talk of smoke doth cloud your senses.

PEDES: Bear with me Sir. The connection is slight but connection there is. You remember last Sunday when I first spoke of your farm? Well, steam engines once rattled its windows and hot cinders twice set the thatch alight. But you'll be glad to know that repairs were made and the cottage is now as good as new.

Phew! I got there in the end.

Chug, chug. Up the incline we go away from the brook

EPHEM: Back there, the Master referred to this as Cotton Country. It surely was so when better squires than I guarded these acres. All around now, I see good husbandry and tended fields, evidence that able men continue the good work of my forebears. But what of the family reputation for rectitude, endeavour and accomplishment that came to and end with the auction sale? How fare the names of Cotton and Beresford?

PEDES: They fare exceedingly well. From 1087 when the recoded history of your distinguished line began, with minor cankers, the family roots have delved deep.

Do your remember your family motto and why the carving of a *bear rampant* was affixed above your door?

EPHEM: Yes, the motto flies from my lips.

Tandem fit surculus arbor – The sapling finally becomes a tree.

And on the moment, those words grip me and I shake with the realisation that this odyssey, dear friends, finally gives me boughs.

PISC: And yonder linnet nests there!

EPHEM: Pedestrian, Master, I, I am so appreciative.

PEDES: But what of the bear?

EPHEM: Yes, the *bear rampant*? It was set there to remind us of that first sapling and of the derivation of our family name. I was taught that the last bear in England was killed at the hallowed ford below our cliff.

PEDES: It was, and that ford and the Beresford's, whose numerous other branches flourished in Ashbourne, Fenny Bentley, Parwich, Newton Grange, London, Lincolnshire and Ireland, continue to flow and nourish. Be assured Sir that the family forest now grows thick and, as I'll show you presently, the modern bearers of the name often meet to celebrate their ancestry.

The bear still dances!

So, it's off this track for a short detour, following the sign to Fenny Bentley.

Can you manage the stile Master? Let me help you.

Now, we'll drop down the hill to cross the Wash Brook on a planked bridge. Can you see the spire of St Edmunds Church? It's a stirring sight.

Come on. Let's run. My legs lead the charge.

Ch-ch-ch-ar-ge!

I'm at it again, aping the antics of my children who I taught to mole jump.

You try it. That's it. Let gravity take your legs and launch yourself into the air, landing two-footed on that delicious mound of soil, remembering not to squash the little nose if the beast pops up to laugh at you.

Try again, this time uttering the famous battle cry 'Mole Jumping!' as you land.

Wonderful! Now you Ephemator.

EPHEM: 'Tis such a jolly and a decidedly silly game, but yonder farmer is tossing his head in uncontrolled mirth, thinking we three must have fled from Bedlam. Let's cross the brook before the men with shackles arrive.

These fields seem familiar. I must have cavorted here as a boy.

I remember this path to the church.

PEDES: Let's go inside. It's full of Beresford family history and has its own Beresford Chapel.

This is the main treasure I brought you to see Ephemator. It's the tomb of Thomas Beresford and his wife Agnes. Your ancestor married well. Agnes was a Cheshire heiress her fortune helping to fund homes at Newton Grange and here in Fenny Bentley. Thomas built Bentley Old Hall just down the lane and its tower, now part of a farmhouse, is still extant. We'll go there presently. The old boy had quite an illustrious past. He fought at Agincourt with Henry V and was one of the 'happy few' but he still found time to father twenty-one children. The fecund couple had an incredible sixteen sons and five daughters. But that was in the days before electric blankets and television.

But tell me, why are Thomas and Agnes anonymously wrapped in shrouds? Why was the chiseller not allowed to show their faces? Most tombs of the period show knights in armour and ladies in gorgeous silks and veils. But these two appear as mere bundles. Was it because of cost? The question has puzzled historians for centuries.

EPHEM: You can ease their quandaries Pedestrian. I recall posing the same question as a boy, my dear mother explaining that in choosing the funeral wrappings of the pauper class, my ancestors wanted to show solidarity with their tenants who were buried in woollen shrouds. Thomas Beresford was a true man of the people who demonstrated his humility even in death.

PISC: Direct your gaze over here Ephemator to this Beresford Stone. Its inscription suggests that it may once have been set above the door or over the hall mantelpiece either in Newton Grange or Bentley Tower. It was found in fragments, restored and brought here in 1879 by a Rev W Beresford vicar of St Chad's in my hometown of Stafford.

And pray examine this. Here's a Beresford epitaph – another sunbeam on our path written by a noble Roman Publius Syrus in 47 BC.

A pleasant companion on the journey relieves the tedium so that it is all one as if one were borne along by a coach and six.

PEDES: Over here Ephemator! This is profoundly relevant to your previous question. You were asking about the reputation and standing of the Beresford family in this third millennium. Here's literature about the reunions that take place each year. Read this poem 'Beresfords' by Ralph Beresford:

Each spring the Beresford Society gathers by the banks of the Dove to share our friendship and love.

You're here to join in the celebrations!

We may all pause awhile to pray and then we're off to see Bentley Old Hall before returning to our railway line for our short walk to Tissington.

PEDES: Close your eyes Ephemator and squeeze in between us like you did this morning. Just a few more steps as we mount the crest… wait for it.

Now! Open them!

EPHEM: Goodness gracious! Let me rub mine eyes in disbelief. I'd recognise those unmistakable contours after slumbering a thousand years. It's my own Thorpe Cloud! Was ever a rising nimbus so beautifully named? Her skirts are billowed in the same enchanted green. Why, I can see the noble summit where Simon and I rattled our wooden swords and coveted the very pinnacle with our competing flags.

She's the most beautiful mountain in the world, the sweet enchantress of Dovedale

PEDES: Yes, she's a fabulous mountain both in fabled name and stature. Nine hundred and fifty glorious feet. Truly a sandcastle for adults. Tomorrow, let's rush to her summit and impress our Union Jack!

PISC: She reminds me more of that ice cream cone you purchased for me in Eastbourne Pedestrian. But hark! I will enjoy the maiden from her hem as you eternal youths rush for her crown.

PEDES: We'll do that Master but now we rejoin the trail and pass through Fenny Bentley Cutting. It's a haven for wildlife.

Just look at those drifts of fragrant flowers on the banks.

PISC: Is it far to Tissington? I'm sorry but I'm feeling a little fatigued gentlemen, the perfumes making me swoon.

PEDES: No Sir. Within a few minutes, we'll arrive at what was the old station and then on just a few hundred more yards to the village and our accommodation in Tissington Manor

You're tired, but be assured Master that I did anticipate your need for recuperation. You'll be happy to note that after our hectic schedule of the last few days, this afternoon is set aside as an interlude for rest and relaxation. So, once we arrive, let me position a comfortable chair for you in the sun below the rose garden and you can doze with only the drone of bees for company.

PISC: Thank you for considering an old man. It sounds an admirable prospect.

But I mustn't drowse too long. After all, there'll be plenty of time for snoozing next week!

EPHEM: Tell us about our host Pedestrian.

PEDES: His name is Percival. He's a Twist. His ancestors came over with William the Conqueror in 1066 and have been in Tissington ever since. Many powerful families have lost their lofty positions, particularly in recent years, the suppression of ancient rights, revolutions in the class system, reckless investments, debts, taxation and the onerous financial burdens of maintaining large houses, all contributing to the demise of feudal ways. Unlike in your day, lords-of-the-manor no longer exert the influence over ordinary people as they once did. Except for the most fawning individuals, you'll no longer find farmers and workingmen tipping their caps in fealty to the aristocracy. Why, even dukes and earls can now wield a spade and Sir Percival himself does his share of waiting on tables in his own village inn!

He still owns a large estate in Tissington but he works hard to make ends meet and has a real passion for preserving one of the finest showcase villages in Derbyshire.

Tissington still enjoys its annual Well Dressing. The event attracts thousands of people each year.

PISC: Sir Percival? What have you told him about us?

PEDES: I've been perfectly honest with him and told him everything, just as I did with 41.

EPHEM: You smile Pedestrian. Angler 41 was an accepting soul especially after we showed him that most singular coin but Sir Percival Twist? How did you convince him that you were not delusional or were not perpetrating some bizarre bamboozlement?

PEDES: With a song in my heart I told him the exact details of our divine compact.

PISC: But Pedestrian, he cannot believe we are resurrected? Surely, he thinks that our appearance is nothing but a masquerade by impostors who will return to the theatre boards next week?

PEDES: True, he smirked when I told him you were evanescent flesh and blood but I think the persuasion and passion of our cause allowed him, for the duration of our visit at least, to suspend his scepticism. He seemed totally captivated by the merits and pure excitement of our adventure and wanted to play his part in its success. Sir Percival resoundingly believes that my narrative will fulfil its purpose and will be an international triumph. Why, he's already confessed he'll commission a blue plaque for his door and order extra glasses for the pub!

EPHEM: I spy the village chimneys through the trees.

PEDES: It's a stirring sight. I first beheld the wonder of this village last winter. Two weeks of blizzards kept me imprisoned in the manor house to survive on Christmas mince pies until hunger forced me here on foot through the drifts. Tissington has a ruddy-faced butcher. His sausages gave me the strength of a snowplough!

We go left here off the trail into the village.

EPHEM: Ah! The Coffin Well and the village pond. Both are as I remember them. A few hundred yards up the lane is the manor you say?

PISC: Such an elegant and beautifully proportioned structure.

By the gate. The man in the white suit and the straw hat. He's collecting money. Is that Sir Percival?

PEDES: It is Master yes. The sign on the wall tells me it's the day of the Tissington Fete. It seems as if Sir Percival, like his neighbour at the big hall has turned over his garden to the coconut shies and stalls and here on our tail comes a phalanx of musicians in the livery of the Ashbourne Brass Band. We're in for a lively afternoon.

Sorry about your nap Piscator!

Good day Sir Percival. May I introduce the two very special people I told you about?

SIR PERCIVAL: Gentlemen! A thousand welcomes to Tissington Manor. Let me shake both your hands. I'm delighted to have you here as my guests. Come in! Come in! No! No! There's no need to pay. Do go up to the door and the housekeeper Mrs Blooms will show you to your rooms. Your luggage came this morning. Once you've freshened up a little, you may like to join me in the tea tent. Say in half an hour?

You'll find our family crest above the door. Three entwined fishes. You should salute as you go in!

SIR PERCIVAL: Two teas for Mr Walton and Mr Cotton please Mavis. Or should I refer to you as Piscator and Ephemator gentlemen? And I know you like to be called Pedestrian my friend. Here's your coffee and a slice of chocolate fudge. My wife made it.

Tell me all about your journey guys. Has Pedestrian been looking after you?

PISC: His attention to every detail has been flawless. We've been attended as kings, the attentiveness and honour afforded to our presence continuing in your own splendid chambers.

SIR PERCIVAL: I'm glad you find them comfortable.

EPHEM: We do indeed. You have a fine home, one that your ancestors would be proud of.

SIR PERCIVAL: I hope they're smiling sweetly on us. When you get back; up there I mean, perhaps you could get the family together and organise a whip round? We need funding for a new roof!

EPHEM: We'll see what we can do.

SIR PERCIVAL: That would be capital.

Now, I must circulate a little and introduce the brass band. Their programme includes an unusual medley of Beatles tunes.

PISC: Beatles? You have us at a disadvantage Sir. We've never heard of such an outlandishly named ensemble have we Ephemator?

EPHEM: Indubitably no. Are they local musicians?

SIR PERCIVAL: No, they're, or rather, they were from Liverpool.

Stuff me Pedestrian! These guys are good. Their facial expressions have never flickered. You've almost got me believing in what I thought originally was one of the biggest cock and bull stories in history.

See you three for dinner in the dining room at 6.30 sharp.

Enjoy the Beatles!

FIFTH DAY

CHAPTER TWO

Divine waters

Thursday. The Feast of St Pantaenus. Evening. Tissington Manor.

EPHEM: Good evening Sir.

SIR PERCIVAL: Good evening gentlemen. I thought you'd like to dine in here. Cook has prepared a selection of cold meats and salad. Please help yourselves and do take a glass of wine.

I'm sorry Ephemator. I mean I'm sorry for staring. It's uncanny. Did you notice the portrait of the lady as you came in the manor?

EPHEM: I did Sir yes.

SIR RICHARD: Well didn't the resemblance stop you dead? Before I came to dinner I was feverishly shuffling through some old inventories in the library and it appears that the lady in question married one of my ancestors. There's nothing unusual in that of course but what is unusual is her pedigree. A parchment tells me she was a Beresford, a Beresford from Beresford Hall.

But wasn't Charles Cotton also a native of that place?

EPHEM: I was Sir and I go there on the morrow to pay my final visit.

SIR PERCIVAL: Now my head is really spinning.

PISC: Pray rest easy Sir for I shall still your vertigo, swearing on yonder crucifix of the veracity of our quest and the names of the men before you. Take heed that we three truly are embarked on a divine mission and before this night is out, I will incontrovertibly prove it. But let us talk first of divine things.

Tell me about Tissington's holy wells.

SIR PERCIVAL: Tissington is indeed a holy place regarded across the world as the mother shrine of all well dressing.

PEDES: That's one of the reasons why I was compelled to include the village in our itinerary.

SIR PERCIVAL: You know our reputation Pedestrian. I remember meeting you first on the last Ascension Day when you were taking photographs.

Tissington was the first place in the country to dress its wells, the customs probably beginning in 1348 when the purity of our water is alleged to have prevented the spread of disease during the ravages of the Black Death. With minor breaks, the villagers have dressed their five wells in praise and thanksgiving ever year, frames of wet clay forming the basis of decorative, mainly biblically inspired tableaux picked out in flower petals. It's a labour of love for the entire village population and everybody takes part. My family have always encouraged and supported the event. It's as though Tissington undergoes an annual baptism, our waters nurturing and replenishing the village in a benign cycle of renewal.

If you'll pardon the pun, you could say that my family are immersed in water.

Tissington is an exceptionally peaceful and tranquil village. Visitors remark on it. I think it's a lot to do with the quality of our water and our reverence for it.

I'm not, unlike you three, an angler but do you know something, I'm haunted by water.

PEDES: A famous author uttered the same compulsive words. Have you read the book *A River Runs Through It* by Norman Maclean?

SIR PERCIVAL: No I've not but I'm utterly captivated by our wells and I regularly take a cup to the source opposite Tissington Hall.

For years I've believed it possesses healing properties like the spa waters in Buxton and Matlock Bath. People have called me old fashioned of course or they've suggested I exaggerate the therapeutic properties of the well to draw more people to the village and to keep my pub's tills ringing. That's nonsense. Honestly, I've a conviction that the water has an energy beyond its chemical composition and I've now found a book that bears that out.

Have you come across *The Secret Life of Water* by Japanese researcher Masaru Emoto? It's fascinating and compelling, blending together a mixture of science and spirituality.

In the book, the author records his experiments with frozen water crystals, his mind-blowing photographs taken through a high powered microscope showing how water molecules at the moment of freezing respond to positive and negative energy. Amazingly, the more positive the energy, the more beautifully formed and synchronised the crystals become, even benevolent words spoken in the presence of water producing exquisite shapes.

I'll show you the book after we've finished eating and I'll show you much more.

Like your presence here, some of Emoto's photographs are beyond belief. He claimed that when, for instance, water crystals form in the presence of music they become synchronistically radiant. How can that be? I'm not a scientist and I cannot begin to understand the recent developments in physics although I've heard of something called quantum mechanics, which suggests that the outcomes of events can be determined merely by silent contemplation. Isn't that weird?

To think that I could go to the well, take a jug of water and silently recite a Shakespearean sonnet in its praise, watching under the microscope as its ice crystallised in poetic symbiosis.

I was intrigued. So yes, I did something about.

PISC: I venture you sought to examine the crystals from all five wells.

SIR PERCIVAL: I did Sir. I did. I took samples from Hall Well, Yew Tree Well, Coffin Well and Hands Well and the new well the village children erect each year and sent them to a specialist laboratory. And I was astonished to find that the crystals from all six wells were as different as snowflakes, each one competing with the other for scintillating beauty. And knowing you were coming, I did something else.

PISC: What was that?

SIR PERCIVAL: Taking instructions from Pedestrian as to the precise location of the iconic Pike Pool on the River Dove, I went there last month with my specimen bottle.

Come on, drink up! I'll show you what I found. Follow me into the library. It's just through here.

Sit yourselves down by the window and I'll get the photographs.

These are the prints I got back only last week. What do you think?

PISC: I have never seen anything so serenely beautiful in all my life.

Look Ephemator.

EPHEM: My goodness! The finest diamonds are dull in comparison.

In golden days, I screwed up mine eyes and the flood of fractured sparks would lave me to rapture. But oh ye unrealising soul! For unknowing beneath the reflective mirror, the outnumbering glints they shone unseen to blindness.

To think I angled for fifty years in that pool with half an eye!

SIR PERCIVAL: Isn't it a revelation gentlemen? The more you probe beneath the surface, the more you realise that the world pulses to harmony and reciprocity.

It's as though each river, like a beautiful woman, has its own grace and signature. I've been collecting samples from all the local waters, the Dove, the Manifold, the Bradford, the Lathkill, the Wye and the Derwent and their crystals are all different, although some of them, but thankfully not many, seem to be misshapen and dull like blighted flowers. Perhaps it's pollution from agricultural manures and fertilisers? Perhaps it's the run off from roads and sewers? Perhaps it's the effect of global warming and acid rain? Or perhaps it's a consequence of aggressive and intrusive fishing?

I took one of my samples on the Wye immediately following the departure of a very rough fellow who had been splashing about in the shallows, cursing his luck and hooking everything except a fish. I had to laugh. After one cast, his fly finished up in his moustache! The photographs I got back from the lab were about as pretty!

But what's your opinion Pedestrian? You've been quiet.

PEDES: I think the more man probes, the more wondrous life gets, each revelation strengthening the certainty that whatever we do, whether it be writing a book, smiling at a child or merely blinking, we can affect all existence.

SIR PERCIVAL: So you do think that words can move mountains?

PEDES: Yes I do, provided they truly reflect the thoughts that begot them.

SIR PERCIVAL: Emoto has a compelling opinion on the power of words. He says that one way to look at words is to consider them as a switch for turning on or off the vibrations for everything in the universe. Or perhaps, he says, words can be thought of as remote controls that have the power to reach anywhere.

You certainly turned on the vibrations with the *Compleat Angler* gentlemen.

And with its heavenly sponsorship, your book will also be a powerful force Pedestrian. Can you cut me in on the royalties?

PEDES: If it runs to numerous editions like the *Compleat Angler*, I'd be delighted.

I am a Yorkshireman!

But what of the sixth edition of our friends' masterpiece published by Marriott in 1676? I believe you have a copy signed by both our authors.

EPHEM: Pedestrian told us about it Sir, but we cannot recall the signing. It's an old book and must be crumbling to dust?

SIR PERCIVAL: No it's not. Now in its fourth century, its bindings are a little creaky and I handle it with white gloves but otherwise it's in a remarkable condition.

I keep it alone in its own cabinet over there. I'll fetch it for you.

PISC: Before I don your gloves, would you please furnish me with one of your modern pens and a sheet of paper?

Before we sat down to eat, I promised that I would furnish incontrovertible evidence of the imprimatur of our mission.

There, now you append your signature to the sheet Ephemator and I'll take the gloves.

I open the book and compare the signatures. Are they not facsimiles of the same hand Sir Percival?

SIR PERCIVAL: They are. I'm amazed. And Thomas that I am, I'm finally cured from doubting.

Please do me the honour of signing the book again with this new date.

And once your book is published Pedestrian, I'd like fifty signed copies to sell in the pub.

Now, I think a celebration is in order. Let me pour you all a glass of champagne.

Sup up. Isn't that what they say in Yorkshire Pedestrian?

Fill 'em up and here's ti' me and me wife's husband not forgetting missen.

The wine's gone straight to my head and got me in frivolous mood. Shall we sing a song? One of my all time favourites?

My wife's called Mary Jane and, bless her, she's from Yorkshire.

Same again?

Another bottle of champagne Mrs Blooms over here! And bring yourself a glass.

You'll know *On Ilkla Moor baht 'at* Pedestrian, it's your county anthem, but what about you gentlemen?

PISC/EPHEM: Yes, we know that one, every verse.

SIR PERCIVAL: Well here goes.

Thanks Mrs Blooms, you can accompany us on piano.

ALL:

Wheer wer' ta bahn w'en Ah saw thee?
On Ilkla Moor baht 'at.
Wheer wer' ta bahn w'en Ah saw thee?
Wheer wer' ta bahn w'en Ah saw thee?

On Ilkla Moor baht 'at,
On Ilkla Moor baht 'at,
On Ilkla Moor baht 'at.

Aw wor a-coortin' Mary Jane,
On Ilkla Moor baht 'at,
Aw wor a-coortin Mary Jane,
Aw wor a-coortin Mary Jane.

On Ilkla Moor baht 'at,
On Ilkla Moor baht 'at,
On Ilkla Moor baht 'at.

Aw'll tell thi father w'en he comes whoam,
On Ilkla Moor baht 'at,
Aw'll tell thi father w'en he comes whoam,
Aw'll tell thi father w'en he comes whoam.

On Ilkla Moor baht 'at,
On Ilkla Moor baht 'at,
On Ilkla Moor baht 'at.

Tha'll sewerly ketch thi deeath o' cowd,
On Ilkla Moor baht 'at,
Tha'll sewerly ketch thi deeath o' cowd,
Tha'll sewerly ketch thi deeath o' cowd.

On Ilkla Moor baht 'at,
On Ilkla Moor baht 'at,
On Ilkla Moor baht 'at.

Aw'm sewer it wor as warrm as toast,
On Ilkla Moor baht 'at,
Aw'm sewer it wor as warrm as toast,
Aw'm sewer it wor as warrm as toast.

On Ilkla Moor baht 'at,
On Ilkla Moor baht 'at,
On Ilkla Moor baht 'at.

Tha'll get a bonny month i'bed,
On Ilkla Moor baht 'at,
Tha'll get a bonny month i'bed,
Tha'll get a bonny month i'bed.

On Ilkla Moor baht 'at,
On Ilkla Moor baht 'at,
On Ilkla Moor baht 'at.

Then yo can coom an' berry me,
On Ilkla Moor baht 'at,
Then yo can coom an' berry me,
Then you can coom an' berry me.

On Ilkla Moor baht 'at,
On Ilkla Moor baht 'at,
On Ilkla Moor baht 'at.

The wurrms'll come an' ate thee oop,
On Ilkla Moor baht 'at,
The wurrms'll come an' ate the oop,
The wurrms'll come an' ate thee oop.

On Ilkla Moor baht 'at,
On Ilkla Moor baht 'at,
On Ilkla Moor baht 'at,

Ahr ducks'll gobble oop the wurrms,
On Ilkla Moor baht 'at,
Ahr ducks'll gobble oop the wurrms,
Ahr ducks'll gobble oop the wurrms.

On Ilkla Moor baht 'at,
On Ilkla Moor baht 'at,
On Ilkla Moor baht 'at.

An' yo can gobble oop the ducks,
On Ilkla Moor baht 'at,
An' yo can gobble oop the ducks,
An' yo can gobble oop the ducks.

On Ilkla Moor baht 'at,
On Ilkla Moor baht 'at,
On Ilkla Moor baht 'at.

Then we sall all be atin' thee!
On Ilkla Moor baht 'at,
Then we sall all be atin' thee!
Then we sall all be atin' thee!

On Ilkla Moor baht 'at,
On Ilkla Moor baht 'at,
On Ilkla Moor baht 'at.

SIR PERCIVAL: Splendid! Splendid! Such a rousing verse.

Ha! Ha! Ha! I hope neither of you guys was buried on Ilkla Moor!

More champagne Mrs Blooms!

PEDES: Please Sir Percival no! Your hospitality has been wonderful and we thank you. We've had a brilliant evening. But I must get my companions to bed. We've a big day tomorrow. It's the climax of our journey. We go to Dove Dale.

We'll set off early as arranged and we may not see you at breakfast but we'd be grateful if your chauffeur could drop us off in Thorpe.

SIR PERCIVAL: It's all been arranged dear boy.

Bed, bed, bed, yes, you must sleep.

Thank you all for allowing me a part in your great adventure. Tissington Manor has never enjoyed such glory.

You're welcome here anytime Pedestrian and do return with news of your book.

In the meantime, here's a final toast to you all.

I'm sure when I wake up tomorrow I'll find that all this has been a dream.

But for now, God speed and goodnight.

PISC: Goodnight Sir Percival and blessings on your wonderful home.

EPHEM: Sleep soundly Sir Percival and thank you.

PEDES: Thanks Sir Percival. Goodnight.

MRS BLOOMS: Who were those gentlemen Sir?

SIR PERCIVAL: Why they were Izaak Walton, Charles Cotton and my lovely neighbour Len Markham.

SIXTH DAY

CHAPTER ONE

Dove Dale

Friday. The Feast of St Auspicius. Morning. St Mary's Bridge, Thorpe.

PEDES: Thanks driver. Sir Percival might be sleeping late today but when he gets up, tell him again that we're very grateful for his hospitality and friendship.

Goodbye!

So, here we are gentlemen on this old bridge over the Dove. It's the most sacred spot on our long journey and marks the gateway into Dove Dale. The river below is the boundary between two great shires.

Shall we step into Staffordshire gentlemen?

PISC: Why, would you look at that Ephemator? The sign.
The Izaak Walton Hotel. I see it's just up the lane at the top of the hill.

Have you been there Pedestrian?

PEDES: I have Master and I dined there with my wife one recent Sunday. The dinner was good and the ale was brilliant – I had a pint of Izaak – but the Yorkshire Puddings – they were so called – were not the poem in a batter we experienced in Eastbourne.

Still, it's a fine hotel and is very prettily set. Anglers come from all over the world to stay there. They have four rods on the river and the bar is quite interesting with its collection of glass-cased trout, pike, bream and perch.

One thing I found odd as I wandered the rooms though was a framed history of your life. It told me you'd been buried in Canterbury, Salisbury, Chichester or some such place. I can't remember the location, save to say that the error would really have put me off the scent. I could have been waiting like a spare part at a wedding in Canterbury for days!

We turn right here up the lane.

How are you feeling Ephemator?

EPHEM: I'm glowing with excitement with a feeling that no reasonable hedge or ditch shall hold me!

I clap mine eyes on my own pastures once more and am elated. 'Tis like the first morn I stepped through the heavenly portal – although the weather's not quite as kind.

If there were a prescription in a bottle to balm, to soothe and to infuse mankind in wonder, it would be distilled here.

Dove Dale!

And look! Look at the prospect before us!

On our journey, you've spoken about your fellow Yorkshireman Capability Brown, but he's a mere sod puller compared to the architect of all this. At times, I've exulted on the turn of a card but no thrill could match this sweet dale

All I want to do now is to rush to my angle rod and raise the trout.

But here's the lovely Thorpe Cloud and I'm in a delightful quandary. My left leg itches to rush to its summit and affix your Union Jack with my right arm. But my contrary limbs covet the fishing!

What shall I do Pedestrian? I'm in a knot.

PEDES: What shall he do Master?

PISC: Bless him, he shall do both. I'll hold your coats and await your return. I'll rest on yonder bench after reading the information on this board.

PEDES: Come on then Sir?

Straight up!

Keep up!

Remember what you shouted when you rattled my door this morning? Immoderate sleep is rust to the soul!

EPHEM: My lungs are billowing like a mainsail in a typhoon.

Tarry! Have pity Sir!

PEDES: Catch up dear friend and I'll adopt the routine I have with my wife when she starts belching steam from her ears. I'll face the summit and hold my cupped hands backward.

Now, you take hold with your hands and I'll pull you to the top.

I'm the donkey and you're the cart.

Just a few hundred yards more and we'll have conquered Thorpe Cloud.

Wow! Made it! Just look at he view!

EPHEM: I'm a poet Sir but no words of mine could do it justice. Sufficient to revel in Emoto's discovery that when we gaze in joy and wonder, we enrich.

I never thought I would enjoy this sight again. Our entire week together is worth this single moment.

Let me hug you Pedestrian in thanksgiving.

PEDES: Soppy devil!

We'll unhook the cart and I'll race you to the bottom!

Watch you don't stumble.

Come on!

Woa! Woa!

PISC: Did you attain the top?

PEDES: We did Master. The view was magnificent but I don't know how we'll stop our excited friend from racing on without us. He saw the panorama of the whole valley, including the heights of his beloved Beresford Dale.

We'll have to fit leg braces.

PISC: What about a leash?

PEDES: A heavy load would be good. I could put some stones in a backpack and he could carry that.

PISC: That's a capital idea. Can I choose the stones?

EPHEM: Stop jesting you two. Rushing on is the last thing on my mind.

I want to stretch every moment to infinity, I want to dawdle, to linger, to meander, to absorb, to savour, to sniff every flower, to recognise every pinnacle and cave, to relish every footfall and to float this way and that like a summer leaf on an eddy. I want to enjoy every second of these precious miles, feeling as though I should drop to my knees and shuffle as a pilgrim with grazed and bloodied knees.

PEDES: There'll be no need for that, will there Master?

PISC: No, we shall go on unsullied as slowly as the snail.

Your Dove Dale is in fine fettle is it not?

I have been perusing the text on yonder board Ephemator and you will be heartened to hear that after concerns about tree felling and pollution the whole dale – all 37,300 acres of it – was bought by a wonderful organisation called the National Trust in 1934. It's now, for all time, God be praised, preserved and maintained in its pristine beauty for the entire nation. People from the metropolises flock here in their thousands but thankfully only footpaths thread its wildness. Cars and commerce are kept at a respectable distance although some anxious to turn a sovereign have been known to set up kiosks and a personage called Donkey Billy once gave donkey rides along the riverbank. Customers tried to coax the beasts onward once they had reached a certain stone but the animals resolutely refused to continue and turned back to their master who was counting his money and brewing tea at the stable!

He must have been a Yorkshireman Pedestrian!

PEDES: William Markham was a legend!

I have the legs of one of his donkeys Ephemator!

Now, the hardest decision we have today is to decide which path to choose on our walk to the stepping-stones. What will it be? This bank or that?

EPHEM: We'll steer left so we may cross the river on the stones.

PEDES: The crossing is one of the best-known beauty spots in England, its image appearing on countless calendars and chocolate box lids.

PISC: It's gratifying to see such a conflux of people in jolly perambulation – and so many young people and children with smiling faces. Their enjoyment suggests a great respect for nature. There is real hope for the world.

PEDES: The youngster with backpacks walk between hostels where they can stay the night quite cheaply. Exploration is encouraged.

But look how that little chap jumps from one stone to the other with his Excalibur stick held high. He cheers as some noble knight. What glee!

Stride out Piscator. Join him and contest the kingship of the stream.

Now you Ephemator. Put your arms round the Master's shoulder and I'll take your photograph.

But stay there, and I'll ask this gentleman to use my camera and take a picture of all three of us.

Steady – steady – we don't want an early bath – now smile you two. Come on, come on, broader, broader.

Thank you Sir I appreciate that.

This chap? No he's not my father. But yes, he does do very well, especially for a man of 417 years old.

PEDES: Well, here we are gentlemen. We head upstream into the wind for home.

Let each step be a benediction.

But in my excitement, I again babble too much.

S-o-r-r-y.

I'll restrain my tongue for a while and let you walk on in silence so you can allow the spirit of this place to fire and flood you.

But sorry, sorry, sorry! It's no good!

The sentences just gush out as flames and torrents, rivers of lovely thoughts welling up, impetuous words bursting forth from my mouth like the waters that formed yonder cave. If I hold the secret any longer, I think I'll inflate and float away over Thorpe Cloud to bounce the heavens. But, on the other hand, if I reveal my plan I'll ruin the surprise.

But yes, that pinprick of admission is relieving the pressure – I can feel it – I can feel it – and I think, for now, I can continue with my feet firmly on the ground.

PISC: You are an incorrigible tease Sir.

EPHEM: It's true Pedestrian! You must have been a donkey in a previous life. You were a donkey with a perennial carrot in front of his nose and you come back for revenge!

Come on divulge your secret.

PEDES: No! Some of that animating gas has been vented and it now bubbles in your own veins. It must ferment and expand there until the moment when we can all three ascend and touch the stars.

No! I'll now enjoy my little dance of victory – diddly, diddly do – that I used to perform after beating my children at tiddlywinks, and leave you both in buoyant suspense.

For the present, you must let anticipation flavour the cup.

Stride on!

EPHEM: This journey just gets better and better. I've just espied a dipper.

PEDES: A dipper? He's my favourite bird. There he is, over there curtseying on a rock. I passed this way in April and watched a pair of birds flying from a nest high in the roof of a cave. Dippers do so love these fast torrents. If I had to come back reincarnated as a bird, I think I'd choose to become a dipper. He flies as a crossbow shaft and bobs and weaves on his rock like a prize boxer waiting to plunge for his dinner. If ever a bird enjoyed his life, it must be the dipper.

PISC: Our way is expertly paved is it not Ephemator? Why, it's just a footpath but the route is even better than our old road to London. And look underfoot. Like the dipper, the paviour must love life and rejoice in investing his skill for the delight of others. Neath our feet, smoothed and locked in unity his hewn blocks beckon us onward and make me inclined to skip and jump.

PEDES: Have you noticed something as equally bountiful Master?

In the seventeenth century, science did not yet recognise the significance of the petrified remains of animals and plants. Palaeontology was then in its infancy. You may not realise it gentlemen, but you're treading on the incised remains of primitive creatures that once inhabited the floor of an ocean lagoon, this whole area we now know as Dove Dale and beyond formerly existing under the sea.

These footprints of lives gone, continue to sparkle with interest and beauty. What more so a man?

I know it's hard to fathom, but come, run you fingers over the outlines of marine worms and molluscs. These fossils were formed hundreds of millions of years ago, the bodies of all types of life forms from worms to giant monsters the size of those cliffs, gradually sinking into soft mud and, over vast eons, turning to stone.

PISC: Your revelations delight and astonish me once more Sir. Verily, in permanent death these fossils speak to us of eternal life.

PEDES: The paviour must be giddied by the joy of sharing. See how his chisel has cleaved a mosaic of ancient life purposefully exposing a glimpse of times gone for all to see.

EPHEM: You quote a time range of hundreds of millions of years Pedestrian. Such a span beggars belief. If these creatures are so ancient, what of the world itself?

PISC: Yes, Pedestrian, can your sophisticated sciences compute an age for the planet?

PEDES: They can Master. It is thought to be some 4.54 billion years old having originated with what is termed a Big Bang that created the universe. Some Creationists consider this view a blasphemous contradiction of biblical teaching but I'm of the view that all scientific discoveries merely add to our understanding of the magnificent energy that drives all things. I think that if you follow the threads of all religions, they all ultimately lead you to the same energising source. You've alluded to this truth over successive days, all the distinguishing but divisive differences ultimately vanishing into one starburst of energy. This is the real Big Bang.

The world is currently in the grips of a global recession, and there's a clash of ideological cultures and increasing religious fundamentalism and terrorism. You cannot have failed to notice in our short time together – you've both read the newspapers and seen the television news – that nations worldwide are suffering. In my opinion, we need a new world order -a more global and metaphysical view on spirituality. I think that is the key.

PISC: I know when your passions rise, you like to crystallise your thoughts in poetry. I read one of your verses last evening that captures your thoughts exactly.

I should like to read it to you Ephemator.

The Faithless Found

Koran-loosed and cross-less,
Your new identity,
Surrendering churches, mosques and synagogues,
And ideology.

You'll find Him not in tabernacles,
Behind shrines or holy screens,
He's everywhere and nowhere,
And every place between.

It's time for revolution,
The scriptured blackboard cleaned,
God is not religious,
All creeds and sects redeemed

Now shed the dimming cloak of rite and rote,
Renewed and blinkered free,
Reach out and join you Faithless Found,
Your hands in unity.

And there's a note at the foot of the page.

A tiny voice raised against the spectre of international terrorism, joining many others, in an upswelling of consciousness against religious and ethnic bigotry. Optimistically, the poem was written with a ripening conviction that the new spirituality that is sweeping the planet will prevail, ushering in a golden age of reasoning, peace, understanding and enlightenment.

You write noble words with great conviction Pedestrian.

We two came to refresh our book on angling but it seems we three have a much broader purpose.

But your wisdom needs no endorsement from us.

Ultimately it is incumbent on man to discover his life source. Once that happens, you will see that all conflicts will vanish like morning vapours. And you are to take notice of this. When you feel a divine wind on your face in a flat calm; when you hear the call of a linnet above the cacophonous roar of London town; when a crust of humble bread becomes more toothsome than a royal banquet and you write sonnets to the grain, when you sniff a poisonous mist and give thanks for your discerning nose and when you see the sun shine on a cloudy day, when, when my friend you do all this, you will know that you're attuned at last to the infinite source of all things. Then, at that moment, it will feel as though the entire universe has been created just for you.

And blessings on your conviction Pedestrian. Your voice may be tiny but its echo reverberates a thousand fold. You must keep on writing.

PISC: Do you remember this gorge Ephemator? In comparative youth, I scrambled to this wild and inaccessible place only once with the aid of stout boots and a wading stick.

EPHEM: The Dove is at its swiftest here but it held some fine trout in the eddies if you could keep your feet.

PEDES: It still holds good fish. I sat here recently on the boardwalk watching rising trout in sweet abstraction. It was even better than fishing.

EPHEM: The boardwalk is a boon to our exploration Pedestrian. If the paviours squirt the milk of human kindness, so too the carpenters who keep us dry.

PEDES: We'll rattle along, coming shortly to the place where in ancient times you Ephemator – in the *Compleat Angler* you referred to yourself as Piscator – first saw the river from the eminence at Hanson Toot.

I have to chuckle at the description of your descent and the remarks of your companion Viator.

'What do I think? Why I think it is the strangest place that ever, sure, men and horses went down; and that (if there be any safety at all) the safest way is to alight.'

I suspect that the man was a little scared, fearing that the acclivity – 'as steep as a penthouse' – would lead to a broken neck or a crushing from his steed.

And can you recollect the remarks he made when he first saw the bridge at Milldale? He asked if you travelled in wheelbarrows in your country, declaring it made for nothing else but a mouse. 'Tis not two fingers broad,' he exclaimed urging on his mount: 'Why I would not ride over it for a thousand pounds, nor fall off it for two; and yet I dare venture on foot, though if you were not by to laugh at me, I should do it on all fours.' Hoe hilarious!

When we get there, I should like to crawl over it on all fours and you can laugh at me!

EPHEM: In this impermanent world, it is very gratifying to learn that the old crossing between Derbyshire and Staffordshire has endured.

PEDES: It has more than endured – next to one other structure – oh! – diddly do, whisper, whisper, change the subject – what a sight! – did you see the flash of the kingfisher just now? – splendid! – splendid!

Yes, the bridge stands proud and is an iconic destination for anglers worldwide. It's as well known amongst our fellows as the Sea of Galilee, although according to some, it's harder to cross. It bears the sign on its gate *Viator's Bridge.*

Milldale itself hasn't changed much over the centuries. It once had a mill but it was long since abandoned. The only acknowledgement to modernity is a splendid toilet block – bless the National Trust! – for men and women. Even car parking is kept at a discreet distance away from the village, preserving its serenity for those on foot.

PISC: I see it in the distance. But may we rest here on the green bank Pedestrian? I notice you carry a sack of foodstuffs.

PEDES: Yes, we'll linger and munch Master, Sir Percival's cook providing everything for a feast including napkins and a linen cloth. I'll spread it on the grass and we'll dine as kings in the sunshine.

This looks a good place. Sit down gentlemen and I'll see what we've got.

Why, will you credit that! Three types of sandwiches all labelled – chicken and curry mayonnaise, crab salad and beef and horseradish – radishes, spring onions and tomatoes, bags of crisps apiece, a bottle of Chateau Lafitte 1933 and three glasses each embossed with three entwined fishes.

I do so enjoy drinking from crystal cups, preferring these to plastic but it's a good job I always carry my trusty Swiss army knife; the one with the corkscrew.

Plop! Cheers! How very civilised!

SIXTH DAY

CHAPTER TWO

Mill Dale

Friday. The Feast of St Auspicius. Noon. Viator's Bridge, Mill Dale.

PEDES: Right men! If this is Viator's Bridge, I'll honour him and run across doggy style.

PISC: Remember not to cock up your leg!

EPHEM: And watch out for that sheep dog. He thinks you're in season!

PEDES: The other picnickers were applauding from the bank. I hope they've read the *Compleat Angler* or they might send for the men in white coats.

Come on, I'll treat you both to a pudding. The lady in the little shop that she runs from her kitchen, sells ice cream.

There! Get your tongues round those.

Let's sit awhile on the bench by the river and watch the ducks and I'll preview the most magical part of our journey.

In your text Ephemator, you describe leaving the river and following Millway Lane to Alstonefield northeast from here. There's now a road that accompanies the Dove through Mill Dale, under the flanks of Shining Tor, right up to the Lode Bridge and the start of Wolfscote Dale. We'll follow that using a footway.

EPHEM: 'Tis a pity that our itinerary cannot encompass a visit to Alstonefield. My family were long associated with that lovely place.

PEDES: I know that my friend and I anticipated your disappointment, paying my respects and visiting the village only last week.

EPHEM: I hesitate to press an answer but does the olden church of St Peter's still flourish? My precious mother, my first wife and Simon are all are buried there.

PISC: I too hope it prospers, remembering that I once wrote of its prettiness.

PEDES: I called there, finding it in pristine order and I sat in the Cotton Pews where your family and you both worshiped all those years ago saying a prayer to speed our adventure. And as I was leaving, I took the liberty of signing the visitors' book with our three signatures, feeling that the spirits of Charles Cotton and Izaak Walton were guiding my hand.

I hope you don't think me frivolous or presumptuous?

EPHEM: No Pedestrian, not at all. We know that you've been empowered, inspired and guided beyond normal understanding and that those three signatures will, in years to come, be as much a part of the history of St Peter's as my family pews.

PEDES: However, my visit to Alstonefield was not entirely taken up with signing books and praying. I did, I admit, have time for a pint! I called in at the delightful *George* and devoured a platter of fish and chips and mushy peas washed down with a pint.

EPHEM: We did once enjoy our carousing in that estimable old inn – didn't we Master?

PISC: Resoundingly so! It was the finest hostelry in Staffordshire and Mistress Gallichan – what a stout woman she was – didst regale us like princes. Do you recall her towering pies Ephemator? My, you should have seen them Pedestrian. Modelled on the contours of Thorpe Cloud and honoured with that nomenclature, her famous pies emitted vapours of beef and onion and sweet herbs that teased and enwrapped you, their alluring tentacles drawing swooning men in from the fields to gorge and savour. So good were those confections that the magistrate proscribed their baking at harvest time lest the fields be filled with abandoned scythes.

PEDES: Mistress Gallichan you say? Why, there's a thing. After I'd scraped my plate I took to examining the many local paintings, photographs and verses that adorn the pub walls. Amongst them, believe it or not, was a note by an angler from Youlgreave called Walter Gallichan. Referring to the Dove, he suggested that she 'must be wooed with ardent persistence.'

PISC: Much like my second spouse.

PEDES: On the wall of that parlour bar, another piece of homespun caught by eye. 'Tha munna werry t'much abaht t'future lad s'long as th'ast 'ad a tidy past.

And by this time tomorrow, you gentlemen, will have had two tidy pasts!

Shall we go?

It's only a short walk to the bridge and we can follow the river all the way.

The route from here right up to Hartington is less frequented than Dove Dale. Only serious walkers tackle all four dales and I'm glad to say that come this evening, you'll have joined my elite club of footpads.

EPHEM: Look Pedestrian! I see a fish rising in the pool below the cascade. Given a rod – oh for a rod! – I could drop my shell fly right on his snout.

Isn't it amazing to think that yonder fish could well be descended from trout that swam here in my day?

PEDES: Yes, it's akin to members of the Cotton family turning up in Fenny Bentley Church like returning salmon.

And talking of salmon, it's interesting to note that some years ago, salmon were reintroduced to this river. Alas, they didn't survive but perhaps the experiment could be repeated? I know the Trent is now much cleaner.

EPHEM: Salmon were absent from the Dove even in my boyhood. I suppose the effluent from mines and mills interrupted their migration?

PEDES: That's been the case for centuries but watercourses are much cleaner nowadays and there has, I know, been a little success in my own county, some salmon managing to run up the Humber Estuary and on to the headwaters of rivers like the Ouse and Swale.

PISC: It would be a noble cause for there is no more illustrious creature in the whole world.

Perhaps we could get the Izaak Walton League of America to sponsor our cause? Would you kindly write to them Pedestrian and explain that I fully support the idea?

PEDES: I'll willingly do that Master. Wouldn't it be wonderful to see salmon spawning again in the redds of Dovedale?

Here's the bridge. We must cross right, back to the Derbyshire side to begin our walk up Wolfscote Dale.

SIXTH DAY

CHAPTER THREE

Wolfscote Dale

Friday. The Feast of St Auspicius. Early afternoon. Lode Bridge, Wolfscote Dale.

PEDES: We follow the ancient sign by this lovely riverside house. What a paradisiacal place to live. It would be my dream home.

PISC: I've told you to keep your belief kindled Pedestrian. Keep manifesting my dear friend and it will happen.

EPHEM: I'd completely forgotten how sumptuously craggy and precipitous these cliffs are. In times gone by, I was occasionally obliged to lose myself amongst this desolation, fleeing from my creditors to hide in anonymous clefts and caves.

PEDES: Wolfscote Dale's precipitous pastures have not changed since the Last Ice Age and they've never been molested by mining or any other industry. Only sheep and debtors ruffle their green blades.

I feel highly privileged to be here especially in such exalted company Ephemator.

And what a ruggedly romantic name. Wolfscote Dale. I can hear the call of the wild in each syllable.

In my home village of Bradbourne just to the east of here, is the grave of a man who spent his boyhood working heavy horses on the family farm at Pilsbury Grange and on his uncle's acres at Haven Grange. Nat Gould left England in 1884 to seek his fortune in Australia and then became a journalist and an author producing an amazing 130 novels all about horses and horseracing. Nearing the end of his life he waxed nostalgically about his old home in Hartington and said: 'I have travelled in many lands but never seen a more beautiful place. It is the one place in England that I look back to as my old home and village.'

Seeing all this, I know just how he felt.

PISC: 'Tis a truly magnificent place and so peaceful. The whole island was once like this. Peace is the natural order.

PEDES: I wandered here last springtime and the scene was made even more enchanting by the blooming of swathes of yellow daffodils. A benevolent team of volunteers planted the bulbs as a prayer, although, as you see, Mother Nature needs no embellishment.

Isn't it all so abundant and radiant?

In one of your poems Ephemator, you said all streams were as puddle water compared to the flow of the Dove. Like Norman Maclean, you were a professor of poetry and trout.

EPHEM: I wrote most of my lines on these precious banks. Pens and parchment were always crammed cheek by jowl alongside hooks and feathers in my fishing satchel and sometimes, when the muse twitched me to scribble, I would quit my angle rod in anxiety lest the precious metres be lost to the wind. I have been known to lay down my line even during the evening rise.

PISC: It's seems that we are all three poets. I've also been moved to write verse especially in my homage to friends. You will both know that when you dissolve the ego and put aside judgements and allow yourself to be carried along on the vast and unceasing stream of consciousness that emanates from the mind of God, you'll catch immortal glimpses of the here, the now and the never ending that will cause you to set down an eloquent form of words beyond your own being.

Oh, I've also known the crammed pens and parchments Ephemator, both my wives complaining about the concealed tearings from letters and notebooks that somehow, somehow, found their way into the foul and malodorous recesses of my britches, there to dissolve in the washing tub in a soup of mucky ink and soap suds.

PEDES: I use an electronic recorder and speak away, not realising that I've forgotten to fit the batteries! Afterwards, in realisation, I write on my hand or cuffs with a leaky ballpoint pen and get ink all over my new white shirt. Then, I'm really in trouble! Once, on a seaside holiday, I was so desperate to make a note of some particularly inspired phrase that I took a shell and scratched out the words in sand, only to see the tide rolling in before I could rush and buy a pen!

PISC: Methinks everyone should write poetry as a distillation of thoughts and feelings. Or, if they've the disposition and talent, they should paint pictures, compose symphonies and melodies or write novels, all as contributions to the understanding and glory of humankind.

But I will impress this truth and urge its recording dear Pedestrian. Every soul has the capacity for individual and meritorious expression. Men like us may compose eloquent lines that will keep the presses chattering for centuries. Others with a rhythmic swish of scythe and knife may keep the grindstones turning. In the league of worth and merit, differentials fade to nought. In this sense, good intent and wholesome commitment are the keys.

Let me tell you a story. Years ago in the time of the great monasteries, the monks at your Fountains Abbey in Yorkshire took pity on a former street jester – a crippled deaf and dumb man – allowing him to quit the dusty alleys of York and to live amongst them in the cloisters. Unfit for most labours, his only skill was in sweeping out the monastic cells and in polishing altar candle sticks. He found his life's purpose in these simple tasks and daily-thanked God for his deliverance mouthing silent prayers as he pushed his broom.

Between services in the great abbey church, he was in the habit of putting aside his broom once his sweeping was done and hobbling to its altar unseen, there to give thanks as only he knew how.

One day, intrigued at the absences of the man, the reverend abbot followed the creature to that holy place, he standing silently in a darkened corner to witness a desecration. For a few moments, he too was tongue-tied, watching in horrified petrifaction as the cripple stood on his head and waved his twisted limbs on the sacred ground. The man was dressed in the garb of a harlequin with tiny tinkling bells on his ankles and toes. He was sweating profusely from his exertions.

Suffused with indignation and mounting rage, the abbot bit his lip and emerged from his hiding place intent on ending the outrage. Forgetting that the jester could hear nothing, he bellowed for the mockery to cease and rushed towards the altar with his arms flaying. But he was stopped dead in his tracks and fell to his knees in awe and wonder.

PEDES: What happened next Master?

PISC: He witnessed something so startling that it changed the life of the abbey forever. A statue of Jesus gently stepped down from its niche by the tabernacle taking a chalice cloth and walking towards the man. With a gentle smile, it laid hands on the twisted limbs, took a chair and sat the jester on its knee, tenderly wiping his brow.

Thereafter, the man performed his homage every day, every monk in the abbey watching bowed in awe and supplication.

PEDES: It's a marvellous tale with a profound lesson for us all.

PISC: I hope my profundities have not the torpor of the homilies that send parishioners a-dozing in Sunday pews?

PEDES: Not a bit of it Master.

PISC: That's meet. I am aware that this is the penultimate day of our journey together. The pressing of our final hours urges me to impart every vestige word to fully accomplish my holy vow.

PEDES: I too feel the promptings of the divine compact. All along I've sought to nourish the taproots of enquiry, seeking to draw out from you both every last gem of advice and wisdom.

I hope I've done it with sensitivity and kindness and with the propriety that your high stations deserve?

EPHEM: You've accomplished you task with outstanding credit Pedestrian and the confidence of the heavenly committee – John Muir, Henry Jenkins, Arthur Neville Cooper, Barclay, Belloc, Robert Louis Stevenson and the rest – has been well founded. They made an admirable choice Sir and our report to them next week will speak of you in glowing terms.

With such an outstanding team of walkers and writers guiding the publication of your manuscript, it's bound to be an unqualified success.

Now, the caves in that high cliff look familiar. This view is emblazoned on my heart for all eternity.

Pedestrian, dear Master, extraordinary friends and companions both … I'm home!

SIXTH DAY

CHAPTER FOUR

Beresford Dale

Friday. The Feast of St Auspicius. Late Afternoon.
Beresford Lane Footbridge, Beresford Dale.

EPHEM: I shall ape your knee bending at Viator's Bridge Pedestrian but not to scurry like a hound. I drop to my knees in a humble prayer of thanksgiving, taking this ounce of my own soil in my hand to praise the Lord.

Glory be!

I'll cross this little footbridge unafraid with my heart swelling.

PEDES: Time changes all things Ephemator so tarry awhile on the other side, letting me explain what became of Beresford Hall.

I want to arrest a crestfalling for greater things than bricks and stones abide.

After you sold the hall in 1680 it was occupied for another 135 years although its fabric slowly decayed. Between 1815 and 1838 it was largely abandoned although the south front continued to be used as a farmhouse and was described as 'in tolerable order' in 1838. I'm afraid twenty years later it was pulled down with a view to rebuilding but the proposals only progressed to the architectural planning stage. In 1905, fellow Yorkshireman FW Green of York bought the estate and, using material from the former cellar and mullion stones from the old hall, he erected a new tower. Although you're old hall is no more, I'm happy to tell you that the tower soars to this day.

I do hope you're not too disappointed?

EPHEM: No Sir. I realise now that stones crumble. Only love and fellowship are perpetual.

PISC: Give me your arm Ephemator and we shall walk on together.

Like your abode on yonder cliff, it would seem that the old mill has also disappeared? But it has vanished without trace. It must have been around here that we would angle in its pool?

But ahead! See the vision Ephemator!

Yes, bricks and stones are ground to dust but our thrusting pike still stands proud athwart the stream.

Behold the Pike Pool. What joy!

PEDES: Surely this needle of rock is the most hallowed and iconic totem for anglers on earth? Readers of the *Compleat Angler* have come here as pilgrims for centuries in quiet reflection and infusion.

EPHEM: And I, a pilgrim soul, am happy to be here once more.

PEDES: Well, let me catch the wave.

Remember my teasing at the start of Dove Dale?

EPHEM: We could not forget it Pedestrian.

PEDES: So let the revelations begin.

Come. I'll guide you the last two hundred yards to your surprise.

See, there's a door in the wall beneath the cliff … and here's the key!

In it goes and turn and – voila! I'm in. Now you both.

Step through and close your eyes. And link your arms in mine.

Just a few more steps.

Now, take deep breaths and wonder!

EPHEM: The Fishing House! Is it a dream? Say you too can see it Master that I may believe the vision.

PISC: It's as real as my thumping heart.

PEDES: It's real all right and it's been prepared to greet us, the present owner fitting it out with furniture and little cots so that we may recline here tonight.
Both the Fishing House and the Pike Pool are called up from the pages of your book as by a magician's wand.

EPHEM: Pardon me if I run to the door gentlemen! And if I have breath enough, my old poem will be instantly on my lips.

I could have written it for this very moment!

My river through the same channel glides,
Clear from the tumult, salt and dirt of tides,
And my poor Fishing House my seats best grace,
Stands firm and faithful in the self same place!

I'm panting and delirious Master. Enter under the inscribed portal – look! – *PISCATORIBYS SACRVM 1674* and our intertwined initials in the self same place!

Let us raise the roof in hurrahs!

And what is this? On the table under the window; a note of greeting.

PEDES: What does it say Ephemator?

EPHEM: It must be from the owner. In a beautiful italicised script, it bids us welcome.

I will read it to you.

Everything has been prepared for your arrival in accordance with Pedestrian's instructions. Under an awning, I've set up a small field kitchen (with foodstuffs) on what was your old bowling green. Toilet and washing facilities are to the rear. Rods and other fishing tackle are under the camp beds.

Welcome home gentlemen.

It's been a long time!

Tight lines!

William

What do you think of that?

PEDES: I think I'm well pleased that everything is going to plan.

All we need now is some obliging fish and we really will be in heaven.

PISC: Words are poor conveyances for our surging gratitude Pedestrian. Our surprise at finding the old Fishing House unbroken is total, is it not Ephemator? You baited us with your secret and although you danced as an impish Rumpelstiltskin, you wove straw to the purest gold. It will glitter for us now and for all men hereafter.

EPHEM: This is a fitting climax to our adventure Sir, your hints and vague allusions only spicing the mix. I've drooled on the prospects of visiting our ancient rendezvous once more but banished such thoughts as a chimera. But the monster banishes his baleful mien and purrs with expectation.

In the full knowledge that I might instantly burst and float back to heaven as a draught of air, might I look under the cots and go a-fishing?

PEDES: I thought you might like an afternoon cuppa and a snack before we wet a line?

I asked our host to provide a box of Belgian chocolate biscuits. They're quite delicious.

Put the kettle on Master.

I know I've repeatedly enquired about your feelings ever since we left London Ephemator. But what are you thoughts now?

I'm sure this is a bittersweet moment?

EPHEM: It might have been. At the start of this odyssey, I knew I would have to return to the site of Beresford Hall. Before our meeting, this certainty made me maudlin and I wrung my hands as some survivor of a battle who weeps over lost comrades on blood–soaked fields. In such despondent mood, I recited a different poem.

No more plum-porridge then or pie,
No brawn with branch of rosemary.
No chine of beef enough to make,
The tallest yeoman's chin to crack.
No bagpipe humming in the hall,
Nor noise of housekeeping at all,
Nor sign, by which it must be said,
This house was once inhabited.

But know this Pedestrian, that all my dreads about the hall and all self recriminations were dispersed upon my meeting with two dear friends, each step-by-glorious-step over these last few days opening my mind to the endless possibilities that abound when human hearts seize the day.

After rather faltering beginnings, with new wisdom and with a zest for the sovereignty of the human spirit that I hope matches your own, I now stride on as a Colossus, my prayers of gratitude at just being here ringing as loud to heaven as thunderclaps.

Instead of mourning the destruction of my old home, I rejoice that its old quoins strengthen the modern tower. Instead of ruing my day of ruination, I recommend the lessons learned and the power of forgiveness, knowing that the contemplation of good things can move planets. And instead of sulking here as a son who is ashamed to lift his head to honour his parents, I feel like ascending yonder turret stairs and, in full voice, singing their favourite song, acquainting them both with the modern accomplishments of the Beresford line and with our scared mission here.

In these few short days, I've changed Pedestrian. Thank you so much and thank you Master for preparing me for a better place

Yes, I will have a biscuit.

Over there. Just recognisable is the remnant sward where I played bowls with father. And here, in my minds eye at least, is mother's leafy arbour. I can fix her now on those summers' days when she would shaded sit, watching her tyro son and his friend Simon casting flies.

Such a beautiful lady.

PISC: God anoints all mothers. They have the potential for divinity, their imperishable love streaming out across the millennia in a matrix that connects all things.

All men should remember their mothers with grace and rejoicing, the memories, one-on-one, thousands-by-thousands stretching back locked, and locked-on to infinity, not time lost but empirically ever adding to the mystical web of life.

Just a flickered recollection of my dear mother Anne glows me even now to a state of euphoria.

PEDES: And I feel the same tender thoughts about my own Ethel Elizabeth. Dead these thirty years, she's still my guide and mentor.

Do you know, the day before she perished, she was anxious about my un-ironed shirts! The love of such mothers fuels the universe.

Now, shall we go fishing?

I'll fetch the gear and give you both lessons in the art of modern fly-fishing.

There are fish on the surface, so we'll use the dry fly.

The rods in your day were flagpoles. Today, you'll find they're more like reeds. The lines, in comparison with the hawsers you used, are as gossamer. And the flies? Why, you'd swear they'd just hatched!

PEDES: I'll sit and watch from a discreet distance, remembering that my eyelid was once pierced by a Bloody Butcher that had a Scottish doctor declaring it the first catch of the season!

That's it Ephemator. Remember that the rod only weighs a few ounces. Let it do the work and keep the rhythm.

Good cast Master! Try again aiming to the top of the rise.

Remember the action of Paul Maclean on the Big Blackfoot and focus all your energies. Synergy and absorption. Become as one with the fish. Swim with them as did chimney sweep Tom.

Wow! You're in!

Well done! Well done!

I'll grab the net.

PISC: What a handsome trout Pedestrian.

Leave him in the river.

PEDES: But what's wrong Master? You wear a sad look.

PISC: I see in this perfect fish the whole of God's creation. I marvel at his iridescent flanks and I catch his eye. It examines me and bores my conscience.

It is soundly pricked Pedestrian.

On the feast of St Athanasius, I did catch a pike and sanctioned his despatch. But you, dear Sir, rescued and liberated the fish in compassion, all the while pretending he was destined for the taxidermist's knife. Later though, in sweet admission, you admitted your deceit suggesting that the image of the fish be wrought as paper and auctioned for charity.

And then in Tissington we didst hear Sir Percival's revelations about the crystalled form of ice from local streams, one jewel from this self same pool sparkling like the sun.

What food for massive thought!

And only yesterday in the Dove Dale gorge you spoke of watching the trout in sweet abstraction, suggesting that such reverie was better than fishing.

All this brings me to a bold realisation.

PEDES: What's that Master?

PISC: It is this. The *Compleat Angler* is an undeserving book.

God forgive me.

I not only renounce otter hunting.

I renounce the cruelty and insensitivity of fishing!

Put the beast back.

I now know why I was allowed to accompany you on this journey. God knows that the admission of no other angler in history would have such an impact.

I have been so grateful of having the opportunity of updating and refreshing my old book. Few men in history have been so honoured. But I need to drastically amend some cruel pages!

I crave the forgiveness of the poor slighted otter and I ask the finny tribes that have endured the sporting hook for four hundred years to forgive this purblind soul.

I weep in confession and with tears renounce the brotherhood of the angle for a more holistic view being content, like you, to just sit here in sublime contemplation by this Pike Pool in contentment.

Lo! Legions of my followers misled! But I get a chance of redemption dear Pedestrian. Through the son of my book – your book – beckons redemption!

And honoured that I am by the naming of the Izaak Walton League of America, I seek their forgiveness also, hoping that my purer thoughts are worthy of their noble works.

EPHEM: I've been listening to your scourging Master and I am shocked and surprised. And pardon me if I don't share you zeal for renunciation. I'm hungry and I have before me a dainty trout plucked from the very depths of my own pool. He'll make a fine supper.

PEDES: Please spare the priest gentle Ephemator for I pre-empted the Master's bright conversion. Fear not for your stomach. Our meal is already sourced. From this day on, we three must be like-minded bonded brothers.

Henceforth, we'll fish with our eyes.

Come, let's join our hands in trinity and proclaim to the world the sacredness of all wild things. Return the fish to prosper and we'll dine on bread and cheese and the finest wine awaiting us in your old Fishing House.

And think Ephemator!

At the start of my mission, the Master spoke to me about the measure of my success affirmed in an undisclosed miracle.

Yes, Ephemator … this is it! This is it!

EPHEM: We three are now one Pedestrian.

SEVENTH DAY

CHAPTER ONE

Bacon and beatitudes

Sunday. The Feast of St Zeno. Early morning. The Fishing House, Beresford Dale.

EPHEM: I know of no more beguiling lullaby than the murmur of my own Dove. I've been reclining here in utter contentment, quietly listening and watching the javelin shafts of morning piercing the windows.

Are you awake Master?

PISC: I am. Like you I have been glowing in delicious torpor, reflecting on our momentous week.

EPHEM: Pedestrian's cot is empty, my nose suggesting he's busy with his pan.

Coil your nostrils round that smell of bacon!

What a sterling man!

Cook, driver, guide, mentor, entertainer and nonpareil friend. He has more than justified his appointment wouldn't you say Master?

PISC: Incontrovertibly yes.

EPHEM: Why then, he deserves our rounded thanks. We should honour and reward him in some way.

PISC: He has already pressed me on the matter and confided his heartfelt view. He wants nothing by way of thanks. When I broached the subject, he smiled and said that this seven-day wonder has been reward enough, suggesting that in the moment of parting his eyes would dampen at the end of one of the best weeks of his life.

But he wants something.

EPHEM: Something?

PISC: He covets only the publication of his book – the story of our tri-adventure. On that score we may help him, presently a glowing report to the panel that tasked him.

With its endorsement, the presses cannot fail!

EPHEM: We'll do that without question but I'd like to show my thanks in a more personal way.

PISC: I will talk to you later about that. For now, we are disturbed.

PEDES: Good morning gentlemen! You're having a deserved lie in I see.

If you'd like to wash and dress, I'll serve breakfast. The bacon and eggs are nearly ready. And I've got muffins, mushrooms, black pudding, sausages, tomatoes and fresh ground coffee.

PEDES: Sit yourself down. I'll be mother and pour.

Breakfast tables don't come any finer than this.

What a prospect!

EPHEM: Gracious friend, it's a picture of salivating nurture and abundance. You must have risen with the lark?

PISC: And you bring the bowery bank to us, filling a vase with a flush of wild flowers.

PEDES: Tuck in!

I didn't want to mention the next few hours in fear that my words might speed the clock.

Suffice to say that our journey together has been one long miracle. I've enjoyed it immensely.

Thank you both from the bottom of my heart for your companionship and friendship.

PISC: Words are nothing without their transport in feelings.

You need only to look into our eyes Pedestrian and see the outpourings of our smiles to know that we also value a wonderful man.

Sir, we love you as a brother.

EPHEM: We do Pedestrian.

PISC: Throughout our time together, I have summoned up all the wisdom of the ages to refresh and now to rewrite our book. I have lectured and hectored at times and my homilies have constantly assailed your ears. But now for one last smelting of gold.

We have told you we love you and you – all of you with a feeling that oscillates every fibre of your beings – must do the same, no reticence, embarrassment, prevarication or fear of a cold returning being allowed to choke the molten words.

Carpe diem – seize the moment – say the words!

PEDES: I love you Piscator. I love you Ephemator.

And my, I just love this bacon!

Another rasher or two gentlemen?

PEDES: No gentlemen, leave those. Washing up isn't in the script. I'll attend to the pots and pans later.

We'll set off now on our final leg. Follow me back through the gate and over the footbridge to the other side of the river.

EPHEM: The Fishing House Master. You can hardy see it through the dense tangle of trees.

PEDES: When I first came here, I squinted and panicked a little, fearing it had suffered the same fate as the hall. It was only after I'd seen its little chimney waving that I realised it was intact.

And yes, I had enjoyed a pint. That's where we're headed now. We'll stop off at the *Charles Cotton Hotel* in Hartington for a final jug of ale.

Through the gate and across the meadow we go.

Turn round and look back. Can you see the tower? It's in a glorious setting.

PISC: The finishing line is in sight. We've ambled a long way Pedestrian, haven't we?

Methinks it a real accomplishment for a man of ninety years.

PEDES: It's inspirational Master! I'm only sixty-five years old but I hope to match your years and walk the Pennine Way again in 2036!

PISC: We just might come back to join you. What about it Ephemator?

EPHEM: Yes, if we can get our holy passports stamped a second time.

You never know!

PEDES: Right lads, here's the *Charles Cotton Hotel.* We'll sit outside amongst the hikers and cyclists.

Would you look at the sign? Doesn't he look funny in that ridiculous wig?

EPHEM: I do indeed. Glad I left it behind or I might have attracted a shearing!

Seeing it's my pub, I'll get them in.

Can I borrow some money Pedestrian? I'm afraid I left my wallet upstairs!

PEDES: That's even more hilarious than the wig. Seems like old times!

EPHEM: I can guffaw about it now.

PEDES: The Beresfords' must have some Yorkshire blood in their veins!

Here's a tenner you scoundrel … and I want the change!

PISC: Thank you again Pedestrian. Our brother has been fully redeemed and will take his place in the sunshine lands. That too is a miracle.

Every objective of our mission has been fully accomplished.

You should be well pleased?

PEDES: I'm in raptures Master.

Thanks Mr Cotton. Now, bottoms up! Here's to life!

Bottoms up gentlemen!

SEVENTH DAY

CHAPTER TWO

Adieu

Sunday. The Feast of St Zeno. Early afternoon. St Giles Church, Hartington.

PISC: All journeys begin with a single step. If they are beautiful journeys, they end in an everlasting stride to growth and perfection.

We stroll on Pedestrian. All strengths to your boots and your searching pen.

And so, we come to the parting. After a gloriously memorable week in your company, we leave for a better place.

EPHEM: It's only just better! Adieu sweet friend!

PISC: We truly leave in high spirits and wish your book well.

Tight lines! But not of the angling sort!

EPHEM: Tight lines indeed!

PEDES: I know we've given up on all that but I can't resist quoting from Norman Maclean's book just one more time

You know what they say Ephemator? You know what they say Piscator? In Montana, there are three things you're never late for – church, work and fishing.

I'll add another. Heaven!

Embrace me gentlemen.

Now be off with you before I'm censured for keeping you too long and I come over all lachrymose.

PISC: Just one final word before we leave … and please, not to look back.

Good luck with the auction of my facsimile pike. We shall have a grandstand view of the proceedings.

You may watch the involuntary nodding of a few heads!

Adieu!

POSTSCRIPT

After the farewells, I return to the Fishing House for the last time, to clean the crockery, dismantle the cots and scour the whole site pristine.

Upon closing the door I turn to gaze one more time on the place where we three brothers slept just a few hours before and I'm stopped in my tracks by a sight as delightful as any leaping salmon. I look up to see the chimney waving once more, my gaze fixing on the famous entwined monograms above the portal, before my eyes, the initials weaving this way and that to encompass my own.

In contemplation of the most extraordinary week in my existence, I stand timeless here bathed in the afterglow of friendship. I wander off in a trance to the banks of the Pike Pool and watch alone but in the company of every soul in creation, observing my favourite bird.

Then I too am dipped to immersion and am lost in eternity, all the songs and symphonies, all the words and canvases of man merging into the rise of one fish.

VALEDICTION

This is the most improbable book since Caxton's first printing – an exploration and reinvigoration of the timeless themes we first postulated in our joint work of 1676.

We are both honoured to have been called to participate in the updating of our narrative and thank Pedestrian for taking on the task with flair, imagination, exceptional literary skill and unfailing good humour.

An exceptional Yorkshireman … he paid!

We commend this book in the firm conviction that its pages refuel a fire we lit all those years ago.

Charles Cotton

Izaak Walton

THE IZAAK WALTON LEAGUE COTTAGE CHAPTER (IWLCC)

Since 1922, the Izaak Walton League of America (IWLA) has been restoring wetlands and streams, establishing wildlife refuges and parks, fighting for cleaner air and healthier forests and teaching outdoor ethics to thousands of recreationists in America. Nearly every major conservation victory bears their fingerprints. When founded, the league chose the name of Izaak Walton because of the ethics discussed in his book *The Compleat Angler*. Those ethics guide us today.

Izaak Walton's Cottage at Shallowford near to the county town of Stafford is an early 17th century half-timbered, thatched building attached to Halfhead Farm estate, which was purchased by Walton in 1655. The estate was willed to provide charitable income for the poor of Stafford – the town where the author was born in 1593. The cottage was first opened to the public in 1923 and is now an angling museum.

In 2003, the cottage was threatened with closure by the Stafford Borough Council, an alerted IWLA launching a rescue appeal amongst its members. The response was so good that it was decided to set up an English chapter of the league as a means of securing the future of the cottage. A meeting of the Friends of Izaak Walton's Cottage was convened and it was decided to amalgamate with the IWLA to form the Izaak Walton League Cottage Chapter (IWLCC). Our objectives are:

1. To work closely with Stafford Borough Council to protect the cottage and its surroundings.
2. To actively pursue memberships in order to perpetuate the ideals of Izaak Walton and the IWLA, namely the stewardship of the land and its resources and the value of wildlife and its environment.
3. To promote an understanding of Izaak Walton's ideals to the public and especially to the young people and children.
4. To work with schools and youth organisations to both ensure more young people become aware of the benefits of angling as a pastime and to promote public awareness of the benefits that anglers and angling can bring to the environment.
5. To develop the museum collection into a National Angling Museum charting the development of the sport.

For more information, please visit our websites at www.izaakwaltoncottage.co.uk and www.iwla.org/cottage.

IWLCC membership enquires should be directed to The Treasurer, Izaak Walton Cottage Chapter, 34 Windsor Drive, Leek, Staffordshire, England, ST13 6NL. IWLA membership enquires can be sent to Mr Robert Chapman, 301-972-7334, Maryland, USA – email bchapman@wan21an.com.

The IWLCC is a UK registered charity No 1101295

PISCATOR'S PIKE – NOTICE TO READERS

The pike caught by Piscator on the Feast of St Athanasius of Athos was weighed, measured, photographed and released. Under the direction of its captor and the author, a simulacrum of the fish was created by paper artist Joyanne Horscroft and displayed in a glass case, information about its capture and the signature and authenticating seal of Mr Izaak Walton appearing in gold letters on its plinth. Through the generosity of Mr Walton who is now re-entered through the Golden Gates, this unique fish will be auctioned six months after publication of this book, all proceeds going to support the work of the John Bradburne Memorial Society* and the IWLCC

*P.O. Box 32, Leominster, Herefordshire, HR6 0YB, England. Email:johnbradburne@hotmail.com. Website: www.johnbradburne.com